Lies, Façade & Deceit:
Life After A Toxic Marriage
Part I

Dee Evans

ISBN: 978-1-7362585-8-3

Rise2Write Publishing LLC

www.rise2write.com

DEDICATION

This book is dedicated to anyone who has Overcame a Toxic relationship.

<u>ACKNOWLEDGMENTS</u>

I give thanks to the Most High God for his Mercy & everlasting Grace. I am thankful for my daily blessing and unconditional love. God never left my side while man did and, through Faith and Prayer I was able to conquer through my darkest moments.
I am thankful for my Mother Robin; she has always been my backbone, my best friend, my support system, my spiritual advisor, my everything. We only get one Mother and I am blessed that she is mine.

Thanks to my unconditional/nonjudgmental Support system. My Family and Friends for Love & Support!

I Love you all! My family is too big to name everyone.

INTRODUCTION
I FINALLY LEFT

Tuesday, June 18 the day is finally here. The day has come for me to pack all my shit and leave my Husband. My heart is beating fast, my heart is pounding. My heart is beating sooo hard I can almost hear it outside of feeling it. I am having mixed emotions about this move.

Do I really want to leave, or can we work this marriage out? Should I stay or should I go? I am really starting to doubt my emotions.

I've been with him for the last nine years. We practically grew together! He wasn't my first love or first sexual partner. But he was my first child's Father, Husband and he was supposed to have been my Last everything.

In my mind I was doing it all the right way. We waited to have kids because I refused to have any children out of wedlock. So, am I ready to be a single mother? I fought so hard to never be a single mother. I fought so hard to not be another statistic in the African American community. But… SHIT! This is Above Me now!

***

He left very early this morning to go out of town. He had a scheduled child support court date with his tied ass baby mama. Therefore, I chose this exact date to leave him. I can't wait to not only be done with his ass but his baby mama drama as well. That woman just won't give it up. I don't even have the energy to waste with even allowing her into my subconscious.

***

Now it's time to get this show on a roll. Damn, I didn't

realize I had so much shit until now. Now I am trying to figure out what I should leave with him or what I should take. I invested the most in this damn House! I am so considerate even during this. I am still going to be fair with what I take.

I'll let him keep the Sectional sofa, ottoman, tv stand, master bedroom stuff, bathroom sets, iron, iron board, microwave, toaster, swifter, hell he can even keep some of the pots, etc. You know what I don't even want to take most of this stuff with me anyway. I am not going to want to hold onto the memories. I just want all my son Kai stuff, my clothing, dining table, carpet rugs, barstools, and of course the flatscreens. I am definitely taking these Flatscreens that I paid for. His ass needs to be in meditation mode of peace in quiet once me and Kai leaves. He needs to focus on why his family just left him. He doesn't need no damn entertainment, like no type of it. Shoot, he is lucky I am not taking that PS4 that I paid for. Yessss, I finally got everything packed up and ready to go. I can drop majority of this stuff off to my storage now.
***

Lord knows I haven't even considered this journey that is ahead of me with moving back in with my Mom. On top of moving back in with my Mom, I am moving in with her and her Husband. The last time I lived at home with my Mother I was still a teenager and I am now 30 years of age. Let's not forget on top of that she was a single woman. The fact that I will now be moving in with her as a married woman will be very interesting. I just hit the reset button on my entire life right now. Although, my Mom is beyond excited for this day. I am looking forward to the support I will have. This will be great for me to have a 24/7

Babysitter. I mean this is the only way I can look at this temporary situation and still have positive feelings. I am not excited about moving back in with my Mom, but I know this is the best option for now.
***

It is now 9am, my Mother and her Husband should be here at any moment to help move my things to my storage. I don't have a U-Haul or a pick-up truck. Between my truck and my Mother's car were going to have to make this work. Hopefully, it doesn't be that bad since I am not bringing any furniture outside of the dinning table and flatscreens. We just may have multiple trips, instead of a one trip and done. That is okay, because my Husband is long gone for now.

It looks like they just pulled up. It is about time. I am so punctual to the point that it drives me insane when others aren't. Welp, time to get this show on the road.

I am now officially moving out and leaving my Husband. Whew! This Shit is real life. I never seen this day ever getting here and it's happening right now before my eyes!

CHAPTER 1

SEPERATION

Damn, this room is smaller than I thought. What the hell am I doing? Am I really giving up living in my own house to move back in with my Mom and sleep in this small ass room with a 3-year old child? Okay, it's too late I'm moved out now. Speaking of that. My Husband should be on his way back in town now. I am surprised that he hasn't called me yet.

Well, look who is finally calling me?
"Where yall at?" Bama asked.
Did this fool just ask me that?! I know he noticed them flat screen TV's missing. He must know that we moved out.
"We not there. I moved out." I told him
"Where yall staying at?" He asked.
"It doesn't matter, were not there." I responded.
"Okay then. You had to take all the TVs tho? I have nothing to watch." He said.
OMG is this really his only concern right now. This cannot be.
"You know I paid for those TVs! They're mine." I told him.
"Aight, BET" He responded before hanging up the phone in my face.
***

So, that phone call did not go how I pictured in my mind. Now I am just questioning it all. Was it ever real? Why am I feeling broken all over again right now? Why was I expecting a different response? Why isn't he crying and begging us to come back home? What is happening right now? Did he ever love me? Does he still want his family? This Dude has proved to me that I just made the best decision by leaving his ass! But this feeling hurts worst right now. My heart is in so much pain. The last 9 years has evolved around his happiness. I sacrificed my happiness for his. He is acting as if he is not even phased by his wife and son no longer being there.

I want to scream, and I can't. I just moved out of my nice 3-bedroom house to sharing a room with my son in my Mother's house to prove a point that seems to have not be proven.

***

One month down at my Mom's. Kai is loving being spoiled by his Mama and Papa. I feel a little at ease knowing that Kai is too young to fully understand what is going on. He possesses such a happy spirit. I want to continue to keep him in a nurturing healthy environment. I am loving and appreciative of the help I am receiving from them both.

I just never seen myself ever moving back in with my Mom to the point that this still doesn't feel real to me. (shrugs) I just want to wake up from this bad dream. I am dying inside every day that I awake and realize I am not lying in bed next to the man I said "I do" to. This is the longest we have ever been apart from each other within the last nine years. Through our ups and down we were still inseparable from each other. How can this feeling not be mutual?

***

It's been a month now and my Husband isn't even showing interest in trying to win me or his family back. I am slowly falling into a deep hole of depression. He moved out of the house we were living in together. He moved into an apartment, and I don't even know where he is residing. He hasn't shared his address with me. I feel hurt all over again knowing that he abandoned our home. I had intentions to return home and now we no longer have a home together. He is showing me in his actions that he doesn't want this marriage anymore and found his escape when I left. I am dying inside.

***

I have become obsessed with checking his Facebook page and his Sprint usage. I am still stalking this man and he is showing me no signs of reconciliation. Hell, I no longer even want his Hoe ass but it's just the fact that he isn't even trying to win me back. At this point I am preparing myself to give him back his phone that he brought me since its on his phone plan. I am so tired of checking his call log and text log. It is driving me insane to know that we are separated, and he is talking to other women. It is not even one woman its several women. This man will never change. I am questioning him about it, and he isn't admitting it. This is weird for him to even deny it because we are no longer together. All he enjoys doing at this moment is pointing the finger at me for leaving. This man is Delusional. This is a Major part of why I left. Does he not understand why I left him?

***

I really don't think he is grasping why we are separated. INFEDELITY issues with No TRUST that we just can't repair. He is not making it easier for me to try to trust him 100%

This man has cheated on me throughout the entire nine years we were together. He cheated before we got married and I blamed it on how young we were. Also, I blamed it on the fact that we were still considered single until we were married. In my mind I was allowing him to get it all out of his system before we get married because I believed it to have been the best thing for him to do. We were so young, still in our twenties. The age and maturity level must be the factor of why he keeps cheating on me. Me and my Husband went to high school together and even though we weren't dating during that time the attraction was always there. Then we reconnected, and at that time we were both twenty-three years old. He was single for about a year from his first child's mother and I was freshly single. I just ended my prior relationship a couple months prior. I always felt like he really didn't get a chance to enjoy and explore women. So, I kind of blamed myself for allowing him so many passes when it came to cheating on me.

***

I still remember the first time that I caught him cheating. I went through his phone call log and noticed a strange number that he was speaking with frequently. So, I blocked my number and call the number.

***

A young woman voice answered the phone.

"Hello?"

"Who is this?" I asked her.

"This is Kelly. Who are you calling me?"

My heart immediately dropped, "Do you know Bama?"

Kelly answered, "Bama, no!"

"Well, he knows you because he's been talking to you a lot later. You don't know this number 404-555-5555."

Kelly paused. "Oh, you mean B?"

"So, that's what he's calling himself now, B?"

"I'm so sorry I didn't know he has a Girlfriend," Kelly responded sounding sincere. "He never mentioned it to me"

At this point I just want to know as much as I can know

about them two, while she is vulnerable and willing to share with me.

I responded "So, how long you been talking to him?"

"We been talking for about 3 weeks now..." Kelly was explaining before I interrupted her.

"Oh, 3 weeks huh? How many times have you seen him? Has he taking you anywhere?"

Kelly paused again. "We only seen each other twice. He came to my place."

I instantly responded "Did yall fuck?"

Kelly paused and mumbled. "Yes, we had sex both times. I am so sorry I had no idea he had a Girlfriend, he told me he was single. You deserve better."

Hold the fuck up. What did this easy fuck just say to me? I know she didn't pull the "you deserve better card" on me.

"Kelly, let me ask you something?"

Kelly answered, sounding confused. "Sure"

"Are you Caucasian?"

"Yes, I am" she responded.

All I can do is drop the phone. This Nigga done cheated on me with a Becky!

"Hello, hello, I am so sorry. If there is anything else, you need to know?" Kelly asked.

I picked my phone up and responded "NO Kelly, you told me enough"

"Well, I hope you leave his no-good ass alone!" Kelly insisted.

"BYE KELLY" I yelled in the phone as I hung up.

I remember this Man telling me just like it was yesterday that he doesn't fuck with Becky's because he doesn't like Becky's. He's not attracted to them and blah blah. Lying ass motherfucker! A man will stick his penis in any fucking

thing. I couldn't wait to call him.
***

"Hey Baby" Bama responded
"WHO THE FUCK IS KELLY BAMA?"
He paused and then responded "I don't know no fucking KELLY. What the fuck you talking about?"
"Oh really, so who number is 347-555-555? You been talking to this White Bitch for three weeks and I thought you didn't even like WHIT…E"
Bama interrupted "Kelly a fucking Lie! I aint fuck that White Bitch"
"Bama, why would this woman lie to me?"
"Bitches lie every day. She trying to get under your skin and you letting her. I'm pulling up right now anyway." Bama said as he hung up the phone.
***

At this point I am tired of this Nigga. I done pulled out all his clothes and shoes out the closet and threw it in the living room. I poured bleach all over his shit, from his Timberland boots to his Polo outfits, etc. I just snapped because Kelly aint lying. What he doesn't realize is I have the call and text log. This woman aint lie to me. Yes, she could have exaggerated the story, but she didn't exaggerate shit about their couple of interactions.
***

Bama opens the door and yells at the top of his lungs as soon as he realizes all his belongings were in the living room buried in bleach. "WHAT THE FUCK IS WRONG WITH YOU. ARE YOU FUCKING CRAZY?"
"Oh, MOTHERFUCKER I aint show you crazy yet! You cheat on me with a Becky Bitch! How in the fuck and what in the Fuck! I been holding your ass down and you go out

and cheat on me" I then shoved the printed call and text log in his face.

Bama dropped to the ground on his knees. "Babe, I fucked up! I am sorry! It only happened once. Babe, I love you!"

"Oh, now you want to admit it. Pathetic ass" I stormed into our room and slammed the door.

Bama followed me in the room with tears in his eyes. "Baby, I fucked up. What you want me to do. I'm not trying to hurt you. You mean everything to me. I can't lose you Baby!" Bama explained.

"Block that bitch now! That's what the fuck you can do. Was her pussy better than mine?"

"Hell, no Baby! I was just curious that's all. The bitch was boring Babe. I felt so bad. I was trying to leave it behind me." He answered.

"You felt bad, but you fucked her twice? Make it make sense Bama" I yelled in his face.

"Baby, you all I have! I am blocking her right now. I don't give a fuck about that Bitch. She was whack Baby, I'm so sorry" Bama expressed than grabbed me closely and gave me a tight hug. I felt the tears rolling down his face. I felt his sincerity. I love this man; I felt his pain. I can't let him go over this woman who he just met three weeks ago. This is my man and future Husband.

Bama released me from the tight grip hug and then started undressing me with kisses all over my body. We made love so passionate that night. I just knew I was pregnant the next morning.

***

As I reflect…...That incident was just the first toxic one of many more to come. In that moment I revealed how weak I was for him. I revealed how unconditional my love was

for him. He knew in that moment he had me. The trust was never regained, and my heart was never whole from the moment moving forward in our relationship.
***
Now let's fast forward to the breaking point of today.

I'm noticing my Husband is becoming more distant from me. It seems like he is disgusted by everything I do or say to him. It feels like he is purposely attacking me for no reason. He is treating me so differently like he doesn't want me anymore. We are barely having sex and he loves sex. So, why are we barely touching each other? Our intimacy is at an all-time low. He is starting to feel like a stranger in my house. So, who can this bitch be now? This is all I keep asking myself. I am beyond tired of dealing with the infidelities. I scare and run one bitch away and two more pop up. I am so Sick of this SHIT.

I don't want to face this again. This time I can't even face it. I am tired of investigating and researching bitches for clues. At this point I am praying and leaving it to God because I am one step away from killing this Man. I have a baby boy to raise. I love my son Kai more than I love myself. Kai is what is keeping me calm in this lowest point of my marriage. I am feeling so bad and guilty for bringing my son into this world with a Father like Bama. I must live with this guilt because I knew his Daddy wasn't shit and a Hoe. I still decided to have him. I never trust him and always felt insecure about myself and the marriage. Yet, I still begged for a child thinking it would strengthen our bond and save the marriage. Shame on me for thinking that he would've changed.

I knew he cheated while I was pregnant, with Kai because he stopped sleeping with me in the middle of the pregnancy and blamed the pregnancy. He also blamed me saying that I was so mean to him and he couldn't deal with my emotions. That was painful enough knowing that he is cheating, and I am pregnant with our child. Finding hotel keys in his wallet and hotel room confirmations in his email. Let's talk about taking me through it during what was supposed to have been our pregnancy. Even being aware that he was cheating during the pregnancy. I assumed it would have stopped once our son was born. I believed it was really me and he was going to stop. After I had our son, I experienced post-partum depression really bad. For the first time he was there for me and our son during that time period. He did a great job with taking care of Kai and me. I believed during that time period that I had gained my Husband back and we would be having a healthy marriage and happy family now.

Until, I discovered he cheated again. In my mind I assumed it was another woman that he had started seeing. Once again, I searched through his call and text log. I discovered a new number that he has been talking to a lot. Instantly my heart feels overwhelmed. All I can think in my mind is here we go again. My Husband must really have a problem. This is mental at this point and he may indeed have a sex problem. I am so tired of this I don't even have the energy to confront him anymore. He has broken me, mentally, spiritually, and emotionally at this point. I am so in love with being a wife and having a family. I just can't picture my life without him. He gave me a taste of what happiness can be if he just does right. I don't have the fight in me anymore.

***

God has a way of revealing things to you. He will keep

showing you signs to your face, until you are ready to face it. This day I kept trying to escape from facing finally happened. I remember this morning so clearly.

***

Bama just got home from work and he jumped in the shower. I usually be on my way out the door when he is coming home because he works overnight, and I work the morning shift. That morning I was working from home all day and didn't have any scheduled meetings. I was still in the bed and his phone goes off. All I can think is "who the fuck is texting him"

I instantly hoped up out the bed to reach over to his phone on the nightstand. As soon as I picked it up, my heart dropped. I knew it was time to face this. I already knew he was cheating. I just didn't have the evidence and didn't want to even find the evidence.

The text read from an unsaved number "Good morning knucklehead." I then grabbed my work phone and started calling the number block. She wouldn't answer. I called the number at least 20 times. Then she finally answered.

I instantly yelled into the phone "Why the fuck is you calling my Husband knucklehead bitch?"

She responded with laughter "Why are you so mad" She kept laughing as it was all a joke to her.

Her laughter confirmed to me that she knew he was a married man. She didn't have much to say outside of the laughing. That couldn't of have irritated me more. It made me loose it and I just blacked out on the phone with her. I can't even remember everything that I said before hanging up in her face.

My Husband is still in the shower not aware of what awaits him when he steps out the shower. I just kept replaying in my head how I wanted to respond. If I wanted to do the scene from one of Tyler perry's movies on his ass with the baby oil. I just kept pacing back in forth in front of the bathroom door.

***

The water has finally stopped. I am started to feel anxious. He finally opens the bathroom door. I am all in his face on my tippy toes. Mind you he is 6'2 and I am 5'2.

The first thing that came out my mouth is "Who the fuck is this bitch texting you, Good morning Knucklehead" I threw his new iPhone against the wall to break it. The screen did break and cracked bad.

"Damn, I knew I should've taken my phone in the bathroom. I had a bad feeling" my Husband said while trying to restrain me from hitting him.

"ARE YOU FUCKING SERIOUS! CALL THE BITCH BACK NOW" I yelled to him.

"No! I aint calling nobody back! Why the fuck you are going through my phone. Get the fuck out of my face!" he yelled.

First time he wasn't apologetic, sympathetic, or empathetic in this situation. He was caught red handed by his Mistress text message and he has yet to apologize to me. This was different for me. I wasn't used to this. I started to feel powerless. I started to feel like if I lost this battle and the Mistress who was laughing on the phone has won this fight. After all she was laughing at me the entire time on the call. Now it has me wondering. What the hell does she know that I don't know?

"BAMA! WHY YOU KEEP CHEATING ON ME? WHO IS THIS BITCH?" I'm yelling as I am punching him in the chest.

He then grabbed me from hitting him and walked down the stairs, as I followed behind him and said "I haven't been happy in while with you. You treat me like a child, and it's just not fun no more."

I couldn't help but pause in silence because what the hell is, he trying to tell me right now. Is he trying to blame me yet again for cheating, but this time it is sounding a little different? Its sounding like he doesn't want to be with me anymore and I just caught him cheating.

I finally built the courage to respond to what he just revealed to me. "So, you weren't happy? Is that what you are saying? I haven't been making you happy?" I asked him, scared for the reality of his response.

"Yes, that's right. I'm not happy. It's like we not best-friends anymore. It's not there anymore" he answered.

"Bama, you don't want to be with me anymore?" I asked.

"I don't want to be married anymore. It's like were not compatible. I told you when we got married not to change and you changed." he answered.

"What the fuck you mean Bama, we not in our 20's no more. We 30 now, how can I be the same. I cook, clean, and take care of you as a great wife. How can you say this to me? I put you before me?" I explained.

"Did I ask you to put me before you? No! You did all that because you wanted too. That's the problem, you don't have to cook every day, you don't have to be so domestic to me." He replied.

"Are you serious? I was being a good wife and woman to you. Every man wants a woman that's cooking and taking care of her man. So, that is now a bad thing?" I asked.

"You're just boring. You don't listen to me. You treat me like a boy. I am not your son, Kai is. She listens to me and don't question me. She just listens" He replied.

"So, are you in love with her?" I asked, scared of his response.

"No, I'm not in love with her." He said.

"Well, is she in love with you? Do she tell you that she loves you?" I asked.

"I don't know if she is in love with me. She never told me. I am just trying to be real with you right now. You want the truth and I am giving you the truth" he answered.

I must admit even though he is killing me inside right now I am feeling like I have a little room to breathe with knowing he isn't in love with her but at the same time I still can't trust anything he is saying.

"So where do we go from here?" I asked him.

"I don't know if we need to continue to be married. There just isn't a connection anymore with us." he answered.

I just felt my ego and pride go out the window because that silly Bitch aint going to take my Husband away from me. The immature woman in me raised up and now I'm thinking he has never chosen anyone of them other bitches over me what is happening right now. Why her? Is it really me? Tears just started coming out of my eyes uncontrollably.

"Why are you still here Bama, why haven't you left yet?" I asked him.

"Because of Kai", he answered while looking at me directly in my eyes.

So…our son was literally keeping us together at this point and my son deserves both parents. I couldn't control myself at this point. I couldn't accept what he just revealed to me. This was too heavy for me. I rushed back upstairs and slammed our room door. I wasn't ready to face the reality of how unhappy this marriage has been for me and him. He was the cause of my misery and he just pointed the finger at me. So, this entire marriage falling off has just been my fault. Like he can't be serious.

Now I am just questioning... Why did he propose to me three times and rush the marriage? We didn't even have a wedding. We eloped because when I tried to plan a wedding it was too much drama with his family to agree to our destination wedding. So, we made an agreement that we will just elope since its just about us and no one else. How did we go from that to this? His words cut me deep like a sword. I just knew I was doing everything on my end right. All I could do and want to do at this point is sleep this off because this is just a bad dream. How can this be real?

***

One week passed by of us sleeping in separate rooms and not speaking to each other. After enough thought and missing his body in our bed. I decided to sit him down to talk about our future.

"Bama, we have been together so long and been through so much. We planned our baby. You are going to let this go? We can't work on this marriage?" I looked him in his eyes with my teary eyes.

"I have been thinking about it too. I am sorry for the hurt and pain that I caused. I am willing for us to try to get back to how it used to be." He responded.

I felt so relieved from his response. I just reached over and kissed him, and we started kissing. Everything just felt back to normal for us in that very moment.

***

Now I am feeling like our marriage is getting back on track.

He went from sleeping in the guest room, the sofa to back in our bed. We are back on track with our sex life. He is back calling me and texting me while he is at work. It just feels like the infidelity has bonded us back to the basics. I can finally say that I am happy and in love with Bama again. We are back going on dates and our intimacy is where it should be. I am mesmerized by my Husband at this point. He is such a great Father to our son. One thing I can say he has always been a great Dad. Especially when I was fighting post-partum depression. He really stepped up and held the household down for me. He really is a great Man. I am no longer nagging him and treating him like my son. It really took for him to cheat and be transparent on how he was feeling for me to understand. The truth really did hurt but it helped us grow and restore our love for each other. I am so happy I am starting to have baby fever again. Me and Bama talked about it and were both on board to try to have another one. Kai needs a little sister. In my mind, I do want to wait just a little longer though because I can admit this is starting to feel too good to be true. I have accepted accountability and I am doing my best to be a better wife to my Husband because my son deserves two parents and not only one. Right now, I just want to focus on being a better wife and growing our family. Especially since were both on board with another one.
***

Six months went by and I am starting to have this intuition that he is back on his cheating bullshit. For some reason he is back facing his phone down and taking it everywhere with him. He did stop doing that but now he is back doing that. He did give me his passcode from the last incident. I can go through his phone every opportunity I get. Now this time around he is smarter about it. He isn't smarter than me though. Men will never be smarter than women or sneakier. So, I started to search through his emails and Google search history.

Mind you I did block the last girl's aka "Miss I got the Giggles" phone number from his phone that day I found out about her. I notice he was Googling this name that I never heard of or seen before and he was googling her name with his job name next to it. He was also googling flowers and delivering flowers to this address. Now, Valentine's day has just passed, and he didn't even buy me anything for Valentine's day because he claims that we aren't celebrating these "pagan" holidays anymore. But he is looking for pagan flowers for this Bitch! What in the Hell.

Now, he just recently resigned from that job about two months ago. After dealing with this habitual cheater I started to add it all up in my head. I never knew the girl name before and never even thought to even find out her name. I'm trying to figure out why he trying to send this bitch flowers. I made sure to write her address down and her name. Bama really came so hard at me with trying to throw in the towel of the marriage and give up on our marriage while pointing the finger at me. I lost focus on further investigating who the girl was in the first place. So, it hits me that this Ashley girl he has been searching for is the same Bitch. Now I am wondering if he is back communicating with her because I am noticing the difference in him. He isn't texting me as much as of lately and he just seems sneaky suddenly. I decided that I will wait to confront him about it after I do a drive by this address. I just need to drive to this address first and his car

better not be in the driveway.
***

It's about 4pm around the time I go get Kai from daycare, but I am going to make this stop by who I assume to be Ashley's address. I grabbed my pistol and loaded it with bullets. I can admit I am not thinking clearly right now. I am not mentally stable in this very moment. I am still hurt, and I just don't know what I am capable of if this Bitch is outside.

I just put the address in my GPS, and she is only fifteen minutes away. How dare this Nigga. The audacity to be fucking with a Bitch that is so close to his home. As I begin to enter her block, I noticed the big raggedy blue house with torn blinds in the windows and kids toys outside. So, this Bitch got kids I see! Her neighbor was outside watering his grass. I noticed he was all in my car as if he seen the car before and was shocked, I was driving it. I drove into her driveway and noticed a broken-down van parked and a Honda Accord. I sat there for about ten seconds before just backing my car out of her driveway. In that moment I contemplated knocking on this Bitch door and then I remembered Kai. No one is worth taking me away from my son.
***

I cannot wait to confront this Nigga. It is amazing how the truth always comes out. He really thought he got away with this being that we kind of brushed it under the rug in a sense when it comes to this Bitch identity. Now it must be faced. Bama walks in the house and kisses me on the forehead. "I am surprised your still up?" he asked.

"Baby, please sit down." I asked him.

He sits down with a puzzled face. "What's up?" he asked

me.

"Were you fucking a bitch from your job?" I asked him.

"What are you talking about now? Damn can a nigga catch a break. We were doing so damn good!" he responded.

BAMA, HOW LONG WERE YOU FUCKING THAT ASHLEY BITCH from your old job? Is she the same bitch that texted you that knucklehead shit?" I asked with a serious demanding tone.

"Yes, she is." he said while putting his head in his hands.

"WELL DAMN YOU HOE, HOW MANY BITCHES HAVE YOU CHEATED ON ME WITH BAMA SINCE WE BEEN MARRIED BAMA?! You fucked like FOUR BITCHES on me since we been married" I screamed.

"Its only been HER, DAMN Woman. I haven't been messing with a lot of Women just her!" he responded.

"What the fuck! How is that possible?? You mean to tell me she had all those different numbers. I demanded an answer.

"Yes, and yes" he answered with his head faced down.

"You had this Bitch changing her fucking number to continue to fuck with you. A married man! This can't be the same bitch you were fucking while I was pregnant carrying your child. Did, your ex co-workers knew about this?"

"Yes, Navi DAMN" He yelled as he walked into the kitchen to put his lunchbox up.

I followed behind him yelling "You mean to fucking tell me you had a two-year affair on me with this ASHLEY BITCH? That's why that HOE aka Miss Giggles was laughing on the phone! The joke was on fucking me! The joke has been on me the entire Time!"

"Baby were passed that and this. I cut her off. Didn't we

agree that we going to both fight for our marriage?" he asked.

"Well, did we? Because…." I said before he interrupted me.

"Baby, I love you!" He pleaded with me.

"So, why are you searching for this Bitch on Google and trying to send this bitch flowers then?" I asked him. He looked up at me with that busted/confused look and paused before responding.

"Baby, I cut that woman off and I told her that I am going to make my marriage work. I am done with her." He insisted.

"I drove by that Bitch house today too. Yes, the blue raggedy ass house with kids shit outside. This bitch you were fucking with had kids I see?" I asked him.

"Yes, she had kids but why is this important Baby. I love you not her and why the fuck you are driving pass her house! What the fuck is wrong with your crazy ass. Where was Kai?" He asked.

I felt my spirit leave my body and I just couldn't grasp words to continue this conversation. I just blacked out and started physically attacking him. I punched him in the eye, he grabbed me and threw me on the bed. I raised up from the bed and start swinging crazy. He grabbed me by my neck in put me in the air.

"I'll fucking kill your ass in here tonight. Stop fucking playing with me. I told you that I am not fucking with that Bitch anymore. Either your going to believe me or not. I am tired of this shit! Kai started crying and screaming. At that moment he releases my neck and looked me in the eye and said

"You are fucking lucky for Kai, he saved your life!"

In that moment I knew I had no more fight in me with this man. My life was in his hands. Either he was going to hurt me bad or I was going to hurt him bad. Our love for each other has gone toxic and it's over. It is no longer healthy and will never be. I knew this shit must stop and this time around I need a plan. A plan to leave his ass. He needs to fight for me and feel the same pain I have been enduring all these years. It is his turn now. I am done mentally, emotionally, and physically.

CHAPTER 2

THE DIVORCE

It has been four months of separation. Bama is just not putting up a fight for his family. This is what this Nigga wanted all along. I can't help but feel this way. You just don't fight for your wife and son. Who the fuck does that? Was I that horrible to him?

At this point I have given him back the cell phone I had on his shared phone line. I am drowning emotionally being linked with him and that damn phone. I can't bear to keep checking his call and text log. He surely is getting to know other women. I was able to trace two of the numbers he has been calling and texting.

The first number that I traced was exactly what I expected. This young, ghetto, hood rat looking mess. She looked like she was in her early twenties, no kids, still at home with her parents, freaked out and easy. That sums up what he likes and how he liked them. I was not surprised and knew for a fact that he has been sexually involved with this one. He was spending the most voice/talk time with her. I could imagine what their conversations consisted of. She didn't look too bright but who knows, he isn't too bright his damn self. It would be a match made in heaven. I wonder how long this fling will last with her. It just amazes me how he wasted no time being promiscuous.

The second number traced turned out to be this woman that is a Realtor. At first, I was thinking maybe she was just helping him or helped him find that placed he moved into. Then I noticed that he was still reaching out to her even after he moved. She wasn't the average type of woman he would usually mess with though. She seemed independent and too on top of her shit to waste time with him. Nowadays even the women with their shit together will settle for a nothing ass Dude! The highest percentage of

Mistress aka Side women are these women who are so career driven. For some reason they don't mind being 2nd runner up in their personal love life.

I am the prime example of that woman with her shit together settling though now that I am reflecting on it. I mean let me evaluate myself for a moment. I am well educated with three degrees, a career, and my own consultant business. I mean let's be serious I was the bread winner throughout the entire relationship. I must face the fact that I settled with Bama. I knew I deserved more and better, but I rejected what I knew. I do know for sure that I will never be that woman who knowingly settles to be a runner up, Mistress aka Side woman. I am not mad at any of these women from the past, or present that he has stepped out on me with. At the end of it all it was his decision and choice. He is a Grown ass Man, fully aware of what he is doing. When I think of where we are now, it's like he was waiting for this time to come into existence so he can cut loose and be the whore he was born to be.
***

Why is he not checking up on us? Why am I not getting "Good morning" "how are you feeling" or "how was your day" text messages from him?

This hurts my soul that he isn't even checking up on not just me but his son. Let's take me out of the equation right now. This innocent boy, who loves his Daddy and sees no evil in his Dad. How can you neglect and abandoned him but not them Hoes? Because they are still getting his time. This is exactly why I gave back his phone and got my own phone plan in my name. At this point I just rather not know. I mean he knows Kai is at developmental stage. Our baby just turned three years old. He knows that I am trying to potty train Kai and these are the most important times for his son. It seems like he doesn't even care.

Welp, he doesn't care. He made zero attempts to win me back at this point. You would think we would start completely over and try to rebuild a friendship that he claimed we no longer had. This should be a new beginning for us. For some reason he isn't taking this time to re-learn his wife and fight for his family. In my mind, knowing him I know that his ego is crushed that I left him. He never thought I would've left him. But, how can he even be holding a grudge towards me because I left him. This is what it must be. He is still mad that I left him! Ugh! I can't make any more excuses for Bama actions or choices at this point. There is no excuse for this Sucker!

***

"Nay!" my mother shouted

"Yes, Mom" I answered.

"I just got off the phone with Bama. I know you don't want me in your marriage and business, but I had to call him." She explained.

"So, what did you say to him?" I asked

"I asked him how he was doing and what's going on with you two?" She replied.

"Mom, you asked him how he is doing? It is clear to see that he is living a life like a single man and we aren't even divorced. We are just separated." I immediately broke down in tears trying to understand why she called him.

"Baby, you don't think I am hurting with you. You don't think I am not feeling your pain? I am feeling your pain. He has not only hurt you and Kai but me as well. I need to understand where his head is at because it doesn't make sense to me that its almost five months later and you are

still living with me. He hasn't come over not one time."
She expressed.

The reality of what my Mom just said to me left me speechless with uncontrollable tears falling down my cheeks. I can't even respond to what she is saying because she is right.

"Baby look at me" she asked me as she grabbed my chin.

"Mom, I'm trying to be strong, but it is all feeling like it was in vain. It doesn't feel real right now." I expressed.

"Well. I did speak with Bama, and he is making it seem like you just walked away from the marriage and abandoned the marriage and left him. He is sounding really bitter, angry, and hurt Nay…." She responded.

Before my Mom could say anymore, I interrupted her.

"Mom are you believing what he is saying to you. You have been there from the beginning. Did I just abandon my marriage to him, Mom?" I asked.

"Nay, you left him, and I understand why you left him. I am just telling you that boy is not in his right mind. He was sounding so confused and angry. He really is more hurt about you leaving him than anything." She answered.

"You know what's funny Mom? I know Bama so well; I knew his ego wouldn't allow him to get over the part of me leaving him. I just knew it wouldn't." I explained.

"Do you think he wanted to leave you first? Because I don't understand why he is so focused on that part when his wife and son is not with him? She asked.

"I don't know Mom. I feel like I really don't know him anymore. I thought I knew him. I thought he would've fought for us. I thought the day that I left he would've called me crying and begging. When he noticed his family was gone, I thought he would've lost it in that very moment." I yelled!

"Calm down!" My Mom suggested while trying to console me.

"Its hard to calm down when this Nigga is still playing victim. All he can say and probably telling people is that I left him. But why did I leave him? Is he telling people that he had an affair on me? That he is a cheater and not only a cheater but a sorry piece of shit!" I yelled hysterically with tears rolling down my face.

"I really feel like he is in a state of shock. Maybe it hasn't hit him that you left." She replied.

"Mom, I can't right now. I am going back to my room. I can't have this conversation with you right now." I insisted while holding my hands up high.

Listen to me Nay, I feel your pain and I hate how he is doing you and my Grandbaby. Kai needs both of you, but you must be strong. You knew his ass wasn't shit and you stayed. I always told you that he wasn't your Husband and you still married him." She stated.

***

At this point I'm over this conversation. I just walked away and went back in my room. It's not like I can just drive in my car and go home. I no longer have a place of my own. We were renting the house we had together and when Bama moved out, I notified the Landlord and she put the house back on the market. I am still thankful they didn't charge us the early moveout fee. I mean when I left, I really had the anticipation of returning home to a new and improved Husband. I was not expecting for him to move out only two weeks after I left. When I think about that it just seems like he was already anxious to be apart. How and the hell could he have found a place so fast and on top

of that I don't even know where he is living. This whole situation has really been a slap in the face for me. I am so close to loosing my mind and having a nervous breakdown. I am here with my son in this small ass room with no privacy. I can't even cry in peace here. I don't want my son to see me in such distress. It seems like everything I attempted to do to reach his soul and to cry out for his attention didn't work. Now, I have a new phone and I haven't given him my number. Another failed attempt to get his attention. We are only communicating via e-mail now and he isn't emailing me or reaching out to my Mom about us. You would think that would concern him and it doesn't. Fuck this, I am going to email him now.
***

Email- sent to Bama:
It's funny how we've been separated over 5 months and you're just living your best life. You aren't helping me financially with Kai and you don't even check up on him. I don't even know where you live.
30 minutes later…
Email- received from Bama:
First, you left me, so don't email me this bull shit. I don't even have your fucking phone number. How am I supposed to check up on yall? You don't need to know where I live. You did this to yourself. You walked away.
***

This is the ignorance I am dealing with. He is so focused on the negative and not the root cause of this situation. He is so focused on me leaving him and giving back the phone that he lost sight of what the end goal should be. Unless in his mind the end goal is being a bachelor. I am not responding to that email. I am so drained behind this man.
***

I am now considering filing for a divorce. Bama is taking me for a joke and he really is showing me in his actions that he doesn't want his family anymore. Everyone has an opinion on my situation and are telling me to give him time to come around. It seems to be normal for people to be separated for a year or two. That is not going to cut it for me. I already accepted him cheating the entire relationship. Why should I continue to allow him to be out sleeping with even more women and not being there for his son?

What everyone and Bama fails to realize that it wasn't just the cheating that drove me away. Bama stopped supporting and being the head of the household once he stopped working at the job with the girl, he had the affair with. The financial burden has fell in my lap and he wasn't trying to step up financially. This is what confused me when he was able to just up and move out into his own place. Like how can he afford to pay bills now by himself when he couldn't even afford to pay the entire $1200 rent that we had. I was paying $3,000 in bills including our son's daycare. I stopped working my corporate job behind depression of this separation. I am only consulting part-time with my business. My finances aren't as strong as it once were just six months ago. He is aware of this and he hasn't given me a dime or a penny since I left him towards our son. I mean we are still married on paper and he is still responsible for me, but I guess since I left in his mind he isn't.

I just need someone to talk to outside of my Mom and I can't afford a Life Coach right now or a Counselor. It's like I want to speak with someone but then I don't. I am so tired of people judging this situation looking from the outside in. I am such a private person that no one even knew what I was dealing with within my marriage. The handful of close friends that I do have didn't even know exactly what I've been dealing with. I believe a marriage is solely between two people and the Most High God. I will just continue to pray to God for guidance and strength. I can't loose my faith in God during this because through it all God has been within me.

***

One week later, I finally built up the strength to research divorce lawyers. This is my final attempt to wake this damn man up and if he still doesn't wake up from this then the marriage is truly over. I've been patiently waiting for something that may not happen.

***

Email- received from Bama: *I want to see Kai and I am off today.*

Email- sent to Bama: *Okay, we can meet at the park off the Ave. I can meet you there in the next two hours.*

Email- received from Bama: *BET*

***

We arrived at the park and surprisingly he was there before us. He approached the car and opened the door to take Kai out his car seat.

"Daddy!" Kai screamed at the top of his lungs!

"Hey my boy! I missed you" He embraced Kai and kissed his forehead.

"I missed you too" Kai responded.

My heart was filled with instant guilt for breaking up our family. I just sat in the car and watched them play for about 45 minutes until he sent me an email.

Email- received from Bama: *Get out the car, I want to talk to you.*

***

I got out the car and walked towards them on the playground by the swings.

"What's up?" I asked him.

"Really, just a what sup? When you going to give me your number. This emailing shit is dumb. We too old for this." He implied.

"WOW! Really, its not like you have been calling and checking up on me and your son. I don't even know where you live. You have abandoned us." I replied

"Are you serious, You left me! Let's not forget!" He stated.

"Yes, I left Bama and you moved out the house two weeks later…."

Bama then interrupted me saying "You damn right I moved out after you left me. I couldn't afford that damn rent by myself."

"Bama, how long did you think I was going to be gone?" I asked him.

"You left me; I am not thinking about how long your going to be gone. I don't want to be homeless." He answered.

"This is my point; you are so focused on yourself and that's it. How many bedrooms is your apartment?" I asked him.

"I got a one bedroom" He answered.

"Really, a one bedroom? So, you have no intentions on us living together again?" I asked

"I got what I can afford. You left me in a fucked-up situation" he answered.

"WOW! Unbelievable! You really looking at this situation one sided BAMA! When we were living together you made it seem like you could barely give me half on the rent and now you can afford a one-bedroom apartment on your own." I replied.

"Here we go!" Bama stated and lifted his hands up.

"Here we go my ass Bama. You had that financial burden on me and didn't give a fuck now you just out here moving on and not giving a fuck about me and Kai. When are you going to start helping with him?" I asked. I noticed Bama picked Kai up and started walking.

"My son going to be straight!" He yelled.

"Okay, Bama you know I am only doing my business part-time and not working full time. I still have bills and expenses that need to be paid. You think because I am living with my Mom that I don't still have bills?" I asked him.

"Look I know that, just give me time. I am still trying to get on my feet, and I got to catch my damn car note." He replied.

"I am so glad you brought that up because that is my car! The people keep calling me. My credit score has sunken and I know I caught you up when you started slipping before I moved out." I explained.

"Yes, I know but I am starting over so I am going to pay it. Ima be straight soon and ill be able to start helping you. You do realize you still my wife right. Do you love me?" he asked

"I don't know what love is anymore." I responded.

"I know you still love me Girl! How long you trying to do this separation thing? I was thinking we can do this separation for a year while I get myself together and focus on our friendship." He said.

"That is so funny to me that you are saying this because its been five months now and your actions aren't showing anything about focusing on a friendship. So, what you want to be separated for seven more months so you can

35

continue to live your best life. Maybe have a break baby or bring me a disease? I don't think so! You got me fucked up!" I said while walking away and went and sat back in my truck. He didn't chase me or even put up a fight. He just stayed behind and played with Kai. This Nigga got me so fucked up is all I kept telling myself.

Thirty minutes later... I look up he is knocking on my window to open Kai's door. I unlocked the door and he placed Kai in his car seat.

"Alright lil man, Daddy gotta go. Be a good boy and listen to Mommy." He told Kai. Kai instantly started crying and yelling "DADDY, DADDY!!"

Bama then looks over to me and say "You did this shit. Look at what you did! Get use to this shit!" He slammed the car door.

I instantly burst out in tears because no matter how ignorant Bama was, he is right. Kai is going to suffer the most from us not being together. I also can't allow Kai to see his Mother in such an unhealthy marriage either. How can he learn how to treat a woman if he is raised in a dysfunctional household?

***

Confession, sometimes when I pull up to my Mom's house, I wish no one is home. Being that my Mom is retired she is most likely always home. I know she is going to ask me how the visit with. Damn, I hate that I mentioned it to her before I left. My zodiac sign is a Cancer and I shut down a lot with no words. I don't want to be rude because I know her intentions are genuine. At this point nothing was solved between us. We are still stuck on the same shit. All this time has passed and we both haven't grown through this separation. I am questioning and doubting everything. I don't even know why I haven't even contacted a lawyer yet. I keep going back and forth on how much time needs to pass before I contact a lawyer. Bama shows me more and more that there is no more us. Our marriage, relationship, friendship no longer is alive. He doesn't even look the same, talk to me the same, or treat me the same. I just see the demons on him and around him. I am not even sexually attracted to him anymore the physical desires no longer exist. I assume that is mutual because he hasn't made one attempt to have any type of sexual relations with me since the separation and even before. I wonder if he is back with the Mistress hoe. I am no longer on his phone plan so I can't check the call log to see who he's currently sleeping with. Ugh, let me get out this car and face my mother.

***

"Hey Mom" I greeted her as I walked in trying to walk fast passed her.

"Hey Kai" she reached for Kai and picked him up. "So how did it go" she asked me.

"Nothing changed, no improvements. He seems content with this separation status Mom. I really don't want to talk about it." I answered and went to my room.

***

In these moments prayer and the Bible is guiding me and strengthening me. This whole situation is embarrassing me. I've been so blind to this man for all these years. He has showed me who he was, and I still didn't believe him. I am starting to feel like this is what I get for staying after he cheated for the first time and we weren't married. I finally have two divorce lawyers I plan to contact in the morning.

***

"Thanks for calling the law office of Nick Stives, how may I help you?" the receptionist asked.

"Hi, my name is Navia and I wanted to come in for a consultation."

"Okay, sure. What did you want to come in for a consultation for?" she asked.

"I want to file for a divorce." I answered very nervous.

"Okay, no problem. We have availability for tomorrow morning at 10am. Can you come in then?" She asked.

"Sure, I can." I responded.

"Do you know where we are located?" she asked.

"Yes, I do know where you are located." I responded.

"Okay, please provide me with your first and last name again and the best number to reach you." She asked.

Once I finished giving her all the details, I felt like this moment was surreal and this may really be happening. I haven't heard back from Bama going on forty-eight hours since the park incident. I am tired and just over this whole situation because this is what he is good at. He is good at playing victim and not being accountable for his actions. I am tired of feeling like everything is my fault. At this point I just want to chase happiness and be set free from him. I am growing anxious now to attend this consultation in the morning. I am also ready to get back in Corporate America. I need to get back to work. This idle time isn't helping me or serving a great purpose. My money is running low. I am living off my savings and my part-time business. My mom is still expecting rent, I still have my car note, storage, daycare, etc. This isn't going to cut it. I will update my resume and get back on the job boards later today. Something must shake. I cannot continue to live in misery and loose sleep over someone who is resting well and taking me for a joke.

***

Just left the lawyer office with my confidence on one thousand! I am so interested in seeing how this plays out. This should have him snap to reality and he should see that I a m not playing with his ass. I wonder if he will sign or prolong like most men do. If he doesn't sign in the next 90 days I will have to file again. I just paid almost $2,000 to file the divorce and lawyer retainer fee. Oh my gosh this is real!

***

Five days later I received a disturbing email from BAMA

Email- received from Bama: *Are you thinking about our son Kai. Do you see what you doing to him? You dirty Bitch! I can't believe you filed for a divorce. Bruh real talk at this point, I hate that I ever fucked with you. And I am sure the feelings mutual, but I understand was better off before you came in my life. This is what you wanted anyway and why you left me. Just remember you fucking with somebody that aint got shit to loose.*

How can I respond to that? This is not the response I was expecting from Bama. I just can't keep up with this Negativity with him. We keep back peddling and where not getting anywhere. The reality of this situation is we have a child together, so I am going to have to still learn how to be cordial with him. I am so tired. The pain and damage have been done. It's time that I accept him for who he is and this situation for what it is. It is time for me to be set free!

***

It has now been over two months since I filed for the divorce. We are now almost approaching the ninety-day period of me having to refile for the divorce. I am stressing out because my lawyer has informed me that if he doesn't sign these papers in the next seven days that I will have to re-file and pay another retainer fee. I just paid almost $2,000 and I can't afford to give anymore money. Especially since Bama isn't even helping support our son and everything is on me financially. I just started back working and I am planning to move out my Moms house in two months. I just cannot deal with the uncertainty of having to deal with this ignorant turned dead beat of a Man any longer. I do need this done like ASAP. I do not or cannot understand why he is prolonging this marriage. This entire time of separation he hasn't fought for his family at all. He has failed to apologize to me. He has failed to take accountability and ownership of his actions. He has failed to step up as a Father to his son. He has failed to take me on a date. He has failed to buy me a rose, flowers, anything. He has just failed me during this separation process. He has shown me in his actions that he is happy with loosing me and his family. He curses me out every chance that he gets. It feels like he wants me to loose my mind behind his constant verbal abuse and I am so tired of it.

I have no idea what he has his family thinking. Even his family has turned their backs on me and Kai. It is so amazing how it doesn't matter how wrong a man can be his family will ride with him. To neglect and abandoned my son who shares their same blood line really gets me and at this point I can careless to address it. As long as my son has my Mother and my family, he will be okay and well taken care of. They can all kick rocks at this point because I am over them all!

***

Email- sent to Bama:

Wow, so u gone drag this process out I see.

Email- received from Bama:

No, I'm not. I don't care about being married to you Navia. You don't even exist to me AT ALL. Like I said and told your lawyer I'll get to it. Have a good day.

Email- sent to Bama:

Great, so make sure you go by my lawyer office and complete the paperwork and sign up for the parenting class while you're at it.

Email- received from Bama:

I'm NOT taking no damn parenting class so you can miss me with that.

Email- sent to Bama:

We both have too. Its required in this state. It's a four-hour class dealing with co-parenting after a divorce.

Email- received from Bama:

Bruh, I fucking hate you!

***

I am so tired of this ignorant Man! The resentment I have for him is turning into hate. I need a word with the Lord. So, I knelt on the ground and talked to the Most High God. "Lord, please forgive me for holding onto hate for this man. Lord, please restore my heart... I don't want to hate this man because we have a son together and I did once love this man Lord. Lord!! Please help me! Please heal me Lord! Please heal my heart! I am your daughter Lord! I am a child of yours God! Your child is hurting and cannot bare anymore! When, I married this man I never imagined us ever getting to this point. I gave this man all of me Lord. I am so Sorry Lord for putting him before you. I am so sorry for ignoring all the signs you presented to me. I am so sorry for trusting in him and not you Lord. This man is still

hurting me, take this pain away from me Lord. I just want to be free from this Lord and I want peace Lord. I need peace! I just want him to sign these divorce papers and do right by our son. Lord I ask for forgiveness! Please forgive me for seeking this divorce. Please forgive me Lord for my sins. I surrender it all back to you Lord!" I shouted while kneeled and tears falling uncontrollably down my face.
***

I decided to reach back out to my lawyer to see if she had any updates from Bama. Tomorrow is the official deadline. Which means he needs to have these papers signed by then so they can be submitted in time. I am starting to loose hope of him signing these papers. I just feel like he will purposely drag this out. If he does then were just going to have to be separated for a while because I cannot afford to invest anymore of my money into this divorce.

"Hi Sally, this is Navia. I just wanted to check in with you for any updated on my divorce case." I asked.

"How are you Darling? Are you hanging in there?" She asked.

"Lord, knows that I am trying." I responded.

"Well, you know the last month he has been saying he is going to come by, and he hasn't showed up. I just got off the phone with him not too long ago. He said he will be here tomorrow morning." She stated.

"Welp, all I can do is pray that he does show up because I can't afford a new retainer fee and I am ready to be done. I really just want to be done." I told her.

"Okay, darling. We will see. I will keep you updated if he comes into the office tomorrow." She insisted.

"Thanks, so much Sally!"

"No problem, dear" she responded.

***

The day is finally here. At this point I am not expecting him to show. I am just going to be married to him longer. I have heard a lot of stories of people being separated for years before getting a divorce. We may just have to wait.

Text message received from Sally:

He is here!

Oh my God, my heart just dropped! Tears instantly fell down my eyes. I don't even understand why I am crying right now. He really showed up on the last day to sign the divorce papers. This is really hitting me because I mentally accepted that he wasn't going to sign these papers today. I thought we would be married much longer.

I need to call my Mom; my stomach is in knots right now. "Mommy! He is at the lawyer office now to sign the paper" I told her.

"Well, good that's great news Baby. Now you don't have to worry about re-filing. How are you feeling?" She asked.

"I am feeling so hurt Mommy! I cannot believe he showed up to sign the papers! I feel so hurt Mommy!" tears rushed down my eyes. I had to pull my car over from driving.

"Aww Baby, I know you still hurting Baby. But this is what you wanted right?" she asked.

"Yes, it's what I wanted but it feels so bittersweet Mom. I am just in shock that its almost officially over. That all. Yes, this is what is best for me." I responded.

"I understand you are feeling a little down, but this is for the best. God will send you the right man in time. Bama was never the right Man! Count your blessing and go get Kai and drive safe." She insisted before hanging up.

***

Text message received from Sally:

Okay, he just signed the papers and left. I will email you the next court date for you to go in front of the judge.
Text message sent to Sally:
Thanks Sally.
***

I just walked out of the courtroom and I am officially divorced! This moment is too surreal for me right now. I can't believe I am officially free from Bama! I am no longer his wife. WOW! I am a free woman now. I don't know if I should be shouting or crying right now. Of course, he didn't show up to the hearing. My lawyer advised me that this was the quickest divorce hearing he ever had. I don't know if I should've taken it as a compliment or not. I mean me and Bama didn't have any businesses, property, or investment together. Well, not outside of the vehicle that he is still driving and according to the court documents he is supposed to switch that over to his name within the next thirty days. But wow this is my life now. No longer can I refer to him as my Husband or his wife. No longer can I wear my wedding ring. No more am I responsible for him. No more verbal abuse, cheating, neglect, unhappiness. Most importantly no more settling! I am screaming inside!
***

It has been one week since my divorce has been official. As I sit here in reflect, going through a divorce is one of the hardest times that you can face alone. The decision for me to file for my divorce was beyond hard because of Kai and him not being able to experience Mommy and Daddy in the household together again. I had to learn to accept reality and accountability for my role.

In some cases, you not only divorce your spouse but family and friends as well on both sides. I divorced relatives on

44

Bama side, friends on his side, and an ex-best friend on my side. I didn't foresee the hurt from the people close or within our circle going through the transition. Not everyone is going to side with you through the reasonings why you choose to depart from your spouse. It just became a transition of purging for me. No one will ever understand or know what is going on inside those four walls. There are three sides to each story. Only the Most High God knows the truth. Although, we all have our own perception and comprehend things in our own way. The truth isn't revealed until it's time for the divorce. Going through my divorce I lost people I have known over a decade through the transparency of going through my divorce. But, Hey I am now Officially Divorced, and this feels bittersweet but more sweet than bitter!

CHAPTER 3

THIS NEW FEELING

I cannot stop thinking about this encounter I had with this man I met while still working for my old job almost a year ago. He was the owner of the business that I was trying to sign up for our services. This man was the definition of tall, dark, and handsome. He was at least 6'6 and so damn Fine! I remember when I first walked into his business, I was taken by his height. I love me a fine tall man! I wasn't just physically attracted but mentally as well. It just felt like an instant connection for me. He was so intellectual, and he instantly took me by surprise. I was so impressed by our initial conversation.

We started off talking about how my company can help contribute to his business return on investment. He was so smart and knowledgeable. I knew he wouldn't be an easy sell. He isn't like the average Joe I speak with on a regular basis because he knew his shit! Then somehow, we started talking more about how he started his business and he gave me his testimony on how he got to where he is. I was beyond impressed and I was trying to buy some time with speaking with him.

During my visit, I was also awaiting one of my co-workers to meet me at his location for because my co-worker was going to actually be his account manager and just needed me there to make sure his business qualified and to sign him up. It got to a point that I forgot I was even waiting on my co-worker. We talked until my coworker arrived.

Even when my co-worker arrived, we were still engaged in a great conversation about philanthropy and his plans to give back during that time period. I remember it was back to school season. He informed us about his grand opening for his business and his present plans on giving back to the community in which his business was located. He was planning to give away backpacks, and school items to the kids in the neighborhood. I was so impressed with his story and what he was doing within his community. I hold a passion for serving and helping others. I can look into his eyes and see that he shared that same passion.

As our conversation advanced, I started to share some of my goals with him and my co-worker even engaged into the conversation with sharing. He was such a stand-up man on the spot as I was telling him what I was interested in he called one of his friends who was currently involved in the exact thing. He allowed me to speak to him and ask questions. He even gave me his friends phone number for follow up questions and support right on the spot. He was already inspiring me and motivating me within that little time span. He was telling me that I must just follow my dreams and just do it.

In that moment I knew I needed to keep in touch with him. I went out to my car and grabbed my personal phone number. I politely asked him for his number to keep in touch and follow up with him to bounce business ideas. By this time my coworker had to leave, and he left me there still engaging in conversation with this man.

Once my coworker left our conversation switched gears and I don't know how it even happened. We started discussing more about me, religion, my marriage, infidelity in my marriage, different scenarios, situations, etc. I was instantly so mesmerized by him. He was someone I wish my Husband could've been like or would've been.

This man was young, successful, no kids, fine, smart, and overall a good catch. To top it all I did not notice a ring on his finger, but I can imagine how many women approach him and throw themselves at him. He was so humble too!

I stayed at his place of business for almost two hours engaging in conversation before leaving. I seized every moment while I was there. I was still in shock that I shared with him about my Husband's infidelity. I am such a private person and I shared with him somethings that I haven't shared with anyone. I really felt so comfortable in that moment with him that it was shocking to me once I left. He really had me regretting I was married in that moment. He would've been such a catch to date. Overall, it was refreshing for me to see that men like him still exist and are around. Welp, the reality set in for me and too bad I was married. During this time my marriage was doing okay, and I had no reason to even consider doing the unthinkable. Even though my Husband took me through the most unimaginable things I have always remained faithful to him.

***

Later that day I received a text from him.

Text message received from Jayville:

Hey, I got you thinking, don't I?

Text message sent to Jayville:

Yes, you really do!

Text message received from Jayville:

I hope I didn't start no problems in your household.

Text message sent to Jayville:

No, you didn't! You really got me thinking though.

Text message received from Jayville:

LOL. Okay

Jayville was referring to the conversation we had at his business about infidelity. He made it clear to me that once a man starts cheating like that, he won't stop. It was a lot to think about. I knew that would be the end of that

conversation. I just deleted his text thread.
***

Almost a year later, and a week after my divorce was finalized from Bama. Jayville has been on my mind so heavily. I just can't stop thinking about the encounter we had. He was always stored in the back of my mind because he was like my perfect guy. Even though I didn't know him, I felt like I did. I was never able to open up to a stranger in the way that I did with him. I felt so comfortable with him as if I have been knowing him my entire life. Maybe I did know him in my past life. I don't know, I just know that I told this man majority of my business from personal goals, business goals, religious views, personal marital problems, etc. That let me know within my spirit that he wasn't a stranger there is no way he could've been a stranger.

I recently began to even speak to my Mom about him and the encounter. I really need to talk to him, but I just don't even know if he would even remember me. I still have his number in my phone, but I don't even know if it is still his number. I am so happy I never erased it though. I am sitting up on my bed contemplating on texting him today, right now in this moment.
***

"Navia!" my Mom called out to me.

"Yes, Mom!" I yelled.

"I'm hungry, ride with me to this Jamaican restaurant." She insisted.

"Yes, I am sooo Hungry too. Let's go!" I told her.

I was starving hungry and so excited to eat at this point. This Jamaican spot is beyond delicious.

Every time we come to this restaurant its crowded. They're food is so good in here. Its crowded in here and the men are usually thirsty in here, so I always stay focused on the menu and getting my food. For some reason I feel someone watching me from my side eye. I looked over to the left side and there he was! There was Jayville! Like he was right there sitting down eyeing me. I instantly walked over to him and embraced him with a hug.

"I was wondering when you were going to notice me over here. I seen when you walked in." Jayville told me.

"I quit my job and I am focusing on my Consulting business." I told him very excited.

"I actually am about to buy a new building for an event center" he told me. I just felt mesmerized all over again by his hustle, and drive.

"That's what's up, Congrats on that. I was literally thinking about you today. I was going to hit you up, but I didn't because I didn't think you would still remember me." I told him.

"Yes, I remember you. I am happy you are focusing on your business now." He responded.

"Yes, me too!" I told him. My Mom called me back over to the line were waiting in because it was my time to order. I walked back over to her to order.

"Oh, you knew him. That is why he was watching you. I noticed him looking at you. It makes sense why he was looking at you like that." My mom said.

"Yes, I was just telling you about him. He is the guy I was telling you about." I told her sounding so excited. I noticed he walked outside and the lady behind the counter had a question for him. I stepped in and let her know that he walked outside. So, I went outside to tell him and talk to him a little more.

"Man, It is so crazy that I ran into you today. You just don't understand. I was thinking about you and wanted to reach out to you this morning." I told him.

"ha-ha" he laughed.

"What's your number again?" I asked. I just needed to make sure that I still had a current number and I didn't want to seem as thirsty. I was so thirsty, and I really hope my body language didn't display how thirsty I was. Even though, I did in fact still have his number, I wasn't sure if he still had my number in his phone. I sent him a text message with my number and advised him that I will reach out to him later.

***

Three days later went by and I reached out to him.

Text message sent to Jayville:

Good morning!

Text message received from Jayville:

Good morning, can I call you?

My heart instantly had butterflies because I didn't even know how to start the conversation. Oh my gosh, he is calling me now.

"Hello, Good morning" I answered.

"How are you? How you been?" he asked.

"Well, I can't lie the things we discussed that day has always been in the back of my mind and I pondered on. Especially the infidelity part. When you shared with me that once a cheater is always a cheater." I told him.

"Yes, that's true" He implied.

"Well, me and him aren't together anymore. I left him and moved in with my Mom. We are officially divorced. It was just finalized last week to be exact" I said.

"Wow, a lot has happened. How do you feel? I don't know if I should say I am Sorry or Congratulations." He implied.

"Ha-ha, Congratulations, will do! I am doing okay. Just going through this transition." I answered.

"Yes, I understand. Its going to take time. You are going through a mourning right now." He suggested

"Wow, you are right. I never even looked at in that way. I am going through a mourning of a death of that relationship and marriage. So, What's your relationship status? Are you seeing anyone? Any kids? Baby mama drama?" I asked. I have been wanting to ask this question ever since. I am a little nervous of his response in this very moment.

"Naw, I am single, no kids, no Baby mama drama, ha-ha" he laughed.

"Wow, your single with no kids? What's wrong with you? Hahaha" We both laughed together.

"Yea, I was in a serious relationship throughout my twenties and I played the Stepdad role to her daughter at the time for years. Then when we broke up, I jumped back into another serious relationship that lasted up until my early thirties. She had three kids and didn't want anymore." I interrupted him because I was quite surprised by what he was telling me.

"How old are you again?" I asked.

"I am 36 and you?" he asked

"Wow, you look so much younger than that. I mean you are indeed still young. I just thought you were same age is me. I am 31. When is your birthday? I asked.

"Oh Lord, don't tell me you believe in the horoscopes, ha-ha" He laughed.

"Yes, I do because it be on point! What's your sign?" I asked.

"I don't believe in that. It is all BS to me." He suggested.

"Okay, so when is your birthday?" I asked in a different way. This is a must for me. I need to know his sign. So far, I can't figure it out. I am usually good at guessing.

"June 29" he answered.

"Wow, you are a Cancer like me. Mine is July 7." At this point I was smiling through the phone. I was so happy to hear that we were the same sign even though he wasn't a believer in astrology.

It all started to make sense to me why we just connected because we are the same sign! We talked for like an hour that day. We talked about everything. It just feels like nothing is off topic when conversating with him.

***

Two days later of us talking about our perspectives of spontaneous, he invited me on a date to a Waterpark theme park in Orlando, FL. Obviously, I accepted this invitation. I can't swim but I do love water. The irony in this I know. It would be a nice little road trip since the theme park is about two and half hours away from us. I am so excited, nervous, and anxious! This is an official date. Like he is taking me on a date.

"Mom!", I yelled out to my Mom from my room since.

"Yes, little girl!" She responded.

"Jayville, is taking me to the water park in Orlando on Saturday. Can you watch Kai for me?" I asked her while batting my eyes.

"What, you about to go out of town with this stranger? You don't even know him? Are you sure?" she asked sounding concerned.

"Mom, I have his phone numbers, full name, and business address. I am going to be meeting him at his house to park my car there. I can take a picture of his tag and send it to you. I doubt he is a serial killer." I pleaded.

"Well, I am going to need that picture of his tag, phone number and address. Have you done your research on him? Have you Googled his name? You find everything you need to know on Google." She insisted.

"OMG Mom, I haven't done any background checks on him yet. He seems solid, and transparent. I haven't caught him in any lies or red flags yet. Taking this mini road trip will be a determining factor for me." I explained.

"Well, what's his damn full name? I will Google his ass right now. I just don't believe no man that damn fine with his own money and no kids is single. He gotta have someone Navia. Just don't be a fool and have fun. You just divorced!" she stated.

"Yes, I understand Mom. My guard isn't broken. I am just having fun. He really is refreshing right now, and he is helping me get through this transition Mom. This is harder than it looks." I expressed.

"Okay, well I'll watch Kai and you bet not sleep with him or be out too late him." She demanded.

"Bahahaha…hee-hee", I laughed so hard! I knew she was serious as hell and her intentions are genuine. I just can't make no promises Mama!

***

Saturday is finally here! I am beyond excited to wake up this morning. I can't wait to meet up with Jayville. I am so curious to see how his bachelor pad or bachelor house looks since it's a house. I am curious to see if he is clean or nasty. I want to see his furniture taste and I also want to check for in women clues. I am skeptical on him being 100% single my damn self. Well, of course he must have someone that he is sleeping with and date. Its great that our first date is out of the city. I don't have to worry about running into Bama. Ugh! What a loser! Jayville is such a major upgrade!

Damn, now I am caught in a dilemma on which bathing suit I want to wear. This pink one piece or blue one piece. I want to look sexy and classy at the same time. He hasn't seen me in my potential. He still pretty much wont on this date but he will catch me in my natural.

Ugh! I am just going to go with the pink because I can wear my pink cover up with it. I am so happy I still have these long plaits in my hair because they can get wet with no problem. This should be so fun.
***

One hour later I arrived to Jayille's house and pulled into the driveway. He lives in such a nice, quiet, peaceful looking neighborhood. I just can't believe he has no kids or wife by now. I hope he is not on the Down Low. Okay, let me stop thinking negative. He has not shown me any DL signs. I am just so nervous at this point. I have dated and been with the same man for the last nine years. My ex-Husband was a douchebag. I don't even know how to date at this point or even talk to a decent man. I finally stepped out of my car. I noticed his screen door was open, but his screen door was locked. I can hear him playing an old school song kind loud. I'm thinking wow it is like 9am in the morning. He is a music junky like me. I absolutely love music. I wake up to music, cook to music, clean to music, go to sleep to music, etc. He came to the door and unlocked the screen door to open it. I felt my anxiety that

I never knew I had kick in.

"Well, hello there. Dance with me?" Jayville grabbed my hand and started slow dancing and two stepping to the old school music with me. I was so caught off guard I started stepping on his feet on accident.

"We both cant have two left feet, ha-ha" he laughed.

I felt embarrassed and just played it cool and did a fake laugh with him. "ha-ha" I laughed.

He stopped dancing and turned off the music and turned back around to me.

"So, you ready to hit this road?" he asked me.

"Yessir" I replied.

As we walked to the car one of his cell phones rang. He unlocked the car door and signaled me to get in the car while he took the call. I tried to read his lips out of curiosity but then I figured out that it was a business call. He went back inside the house on the phone. As he went back inside, I just started looking around in his car for any clues. I have no idea what I am even looking for. He walked back outside and locked the house up.

"What kind of music do you like to listen to?" Jayville asked.

"I love everything! I listen to everything" I said.

"Oh okay, okay, I listen to everything" Jayville said.

He started playing all the different music genres that he was into from Pop rock, country, to rap, hip hop, trap music. He is really a music lover like me, but he is more diverse then I am.

Oh my Gosh, he just grabbed my hand while he's driving and rubbed my knuckles against his. That was a little weird but sweet gesture. Damn, I am so mesmerized by this guy. I just do not want to fall so quickly for him. He is so intellectual and well rounded. I just ended a marriage. I need to enjoy this wave for now and promise myself not to get caught up. Jayville is like the perfect guy to me at this point. I never met someone like him, and I do not think I ever will.

***

Two hours later we pulled up to the water theme park in Orlando, FL.

"Damn, I haven't been to a water park since Six flags waterpark about ten years ago." I told Jayville.

"Wow, its been that long huh? I love this shit!" he responded.

"Yes, its been even longer than that since I been to an Orlando theme park" I told him.

"Alright, not I don't need you in here acting scary" He said jokingly.

"Well, I do have a confession." I said.

"Aw Shit, what is it?" he asked.

"I don't know how to swim." I answered.

"What! Aint you Jamaican, from south Florida and you can't swim?" he asked.

"I know right, everyone always says that." I responded.

"We still going to have fun, they got life jackets and stuff in here for you non-swimmers." He said.

"Okay, cool" I told him.

We parked and started walking towards the entrance gate of theme park. I noticed when we got to the window ticket, he brought the VIP tickets for both of us. It really put the pressure on me instantly. I love adventure and I am spontaneous, but I wasn't really in the mood for roller coasters and shit. We walked into the park and that's when it really hit me. It hit me that I'm on my first date after my ex-husband. This is the first man that I have been on a date in over nine years. It feels so natural, like I have been knowing him for years.

"Let's do that motherfucka right there." Jayville requested as he pointed at the waterslide.

"Okay, lets do it!" I told him. Inside I'm so scared to do this, because I really don't like waterslides.

As we approached closer and closer in the VIP line for the waterslide, my heart just started to beat faster and faster. I am praying that we get into the same donut hole thingy.

***

"Whew! That was fun!" I yelled.

"You want to do it again?" he asked.

"Yes, lets do it again" I told him

We had VIP wrist bands and this time around there was no delay on our side, so we were able to get back on the slide quicker. After it was all over, he looked over at me as if he wanted to do it again, at this point I'm over it.

"You want to do round three?" he asked.

"Uhuh" I told him nodding my head no.

"I can see it in your eyes that you don't want any parts with it again, ha-ha" he chuckled.

We both kept walking and enjoying the park. At one point I grabbed his hand and we held hands as we walked. We walked, talked, laughed. flirted, and just really enjoyed ourselves.

"Are you hungry?" he asked me.

"No, I am good" I responded.

"You sure you not hungry? I hungrier than a Bitch right now. I'm starving. Let's go see what they got" he implied as he started walking towards the food stand.

"You don't want a drink or snack?" he asked me.

"Sure, ill take a drink." I told him. I can tell he really wanted me to consume something in my body.

We sat down after he got his food. We talked some more and made jokes with each other.

"So, what are you really into doing? I see the theme park really isn't your thing." He asked me,

"You know what, when I was younger it was. I didn't even realize how scary I became as I got older. I really enjoy the beach, boats, traveling, reading, writing.... etc." I explained.

"Oh okay, so I need to take you to an Island or somewhere there are beaches. I mean we could've hit Daytona, instead of here if I knew that." He stated.

"Oh no, its okay. I still had fun. I hope I didn't waste your money not engaging in all the crazy rides and slides. I am sorry if I did." I told him.

"You didn't waste my money. You are okay." He responded.

Whew! I thought inside. I am glad he feels that way.

"Are you ready to head back, since we have this drive?" he asked me.

"Yes, I am ready" I answered.

I grabbed his food from him and dumped it in the trash can. We walked back towards out locker and went our separate ways to take showers. Surprisingly, I came out the bathroom from my shower before him. I guess because I was rushing and didn't want him waiting on me. Luckily, I didn't have to wait for him too long. He came out about 3 minutes after me. When I say he was dressed so nicely when he came out. I was damn near drooling because he is so damn fine to me. I love me a tall as man. Oh my gosh!
***

Almost three hours later, we are approaching back to our city. He stopped by the business that I met him at.

"You know where you are?" Jayville asked me.

"Of course, I know where I am. This is your business where I met you." I answered with a smile. He parked the car and we got out and walked around his location. He showed me the updated changes that were made there. I was impressed at it and felt like a proud Mother about it. Then we drove pass his other businesses, restaurant, car wash, convenient store. I felt like he was giving me a tour. We stopped by a vacant building that he was interested in buying. He put a bid in to purchase the building. It was a convenient store in the past. He parked the car and we both got out. He had the code to enter the store. He was so excited about it.

As we entered this vacant store, he was walking me through describing his vision about the store. Once purchased, he was going to turn it into an event center, where parents can have children parties, baby showers, bridal showers, etc. The passion is his eyes were beautiful. He sold me on his vision, and I was excited for him and rooting for him.

***

"Are you hungry yet?" he asked me.

"No, I am okay" I answered.

"We been together since 9am and you still haven't eaten. Are you not use to eating?" he asked worried.

"ha-ha, what of course I eat" I laughed.

"Okay, well I have this Asian spot that I love we can grab takeout from there" he insisted.

We pulled up to the Asian spot. He advised me to look up the menu and let him know what I want to eat.

"I want to do the shrimp lomein" I told him.

"Okay, do you want anything else?" he asked.

"No, that's it for me." I told him.

He went inside and I decided to stay in the car and wait for him. He came back outside giving me an update on our food status.

"They said it will be about twenty minutes, that's cool with you?" he asked me.

"Sure!" I answered.

He then came and sat back down in the car. We just vibe out to some good soul RNB music. I wish I could remember the name of this singer.

***

We finally arrived to back to his house. After a long day, I decided to go inside instead of jumping in my car and going home. I had such an amazing day with him I still wasn't ready for it to end.

"Would you like something to drink with your food?" Jayville asked me.

"Sure, what do you have. Do you have some wine?" I asked.

"Yes, I do have some wine. Would you like some?" he asked me.

"Yes sir, please!" I told him

He brought the glass of wine over to me. We decided to eat inside his living room versus his dining area. We ate, talked, watched "Naked and Afraid." That was my first time ever watching that show or even hearing about it. I was a pretty dope show. It is about surviving in the wild naked for 21 days.

"Are you tired yet?" he asked me.

"Could you pour me another drink?" I asked him.

"Okay, then! I see someone isn't tired. You want another glass of wine?" he asked.

"Yes, that'll be fine." I told him.

Then we started sharing our experiences, like sexual fantasies, sexual experiences, and so on.

"For some reason, men always want to eat my vagina. I always have homegirls who men want to have a three some with me. I just don't get it." I told him. At this point I am feeling this wine and beyond tipsy. I am usually very private and don't talk like that so freely.

"Oh really!" he said.

"Yes, really. Like I don't get it. I had like 4 different couples ask me. I reject everyone of them." I told him.

"Now, you got me curious" he implied. He was sitting on the other end of his section and he came over to the end I was.

"You got me curious, can I taste it?" he asked me.

I felt not only my heartbeat but my vagina heartbeat. I just nodded my head and answered "Yes."

***

Jayville tall ass is 6ft.6 inches and he is on his knees while I am laying on his sectional sofa, eating, licking, sucking the life out my vagina. He is down there treating my kitty cat like how a grown man should. I came in his mouth at least three times. Once he finished, he got up and just laid on the sectional sofa next to me as if nothing just happened.

"I was just curious. I had to see what it tasted like." He told me.

"How did it taste?" I asked him.

"Tt tasted good, very tasty" he said.

At this point, I am wondering if his dick is little because he didn't even try to have sex with me. He just got up and laid back next to me.

So, I touched his penis and as soon as I did that. He grabbed my hand and walked me into his room. In that moment it felt surreal. Everything was happening so fast. Did I want to pull him away and tell him, NO! Or did I want this as bad as he did? I was feeling so stuck in this moment. My mind was telling me No, but my body was telling me FUCK YES!

As we entered his room, all I could remember is that his bed looked huge and it was so comfortable when I sat down. Then, we both started taking off our clothes instantly. He assisted me with my bra, and I was still feeling a little shock at what was going on.

He then pulled his dick out in front of me and it was not small in no way. We kissed like we were in love and this Man put my body in every position that you can think of. He fucked me so good in every kind of way in positions that I have never even tried. He took his dick out at one point and told me to ride his face so he can eat my kitty cat again. He was so naturally freaky and fucking good at pleasing me. It's like he knew just what to do to please my body. He knew exactly what to do to me. If I wasn't in love before I was in love now.

***

"Do you want to jump in the shower?" he asked me as he gave me a washcloth.

"Yes, I would like to." I grabbed the washcloth and went in his bathroom to take a shower.

Oh my gosh! What the hell did I just do. I wonder if he is thinking I am easy, or a hoe. I instantly felt shame over my actions, but it was the best fucking sex I had in so long that feeling of shame didn't last long. As I finished, I was planning my exit in my head. I did not want to spend a night. I did beg my Mom to keep my son and she already warned me not to sleep with this man. Ugh! She would be so mad if she knew I slept with him already. But, fuck it! This is my life. I am still not telling her anyway. I finished my shower and put my clothes back on.

"Hey, I'm about to head out" I told Jayville.

"Okay, I had so much fun with you today." He told me.

"Yes, I did too." I replied. He then walked me to my car.

"Text me let me know when you make it home. Another man trash is another one treasure" he said.

All I could do is smile and nod at him as I drove off.

Text message sent to Jayville:

I made it home.

Text message received from Jayville:

Okay, have a good night.

***

CHAPTER 4

JaYville

Text message received from Jayville:
Good morning Beautiful
Text message sent to Jayville:
Good morning Handsome
Text message received from Jayville:
How are you feeling this morning? Wyd?
Text message sent to Jayville:
I am feeling ok. Just waking up
Text message received from Jayville:
Okay
Text message sent to Jayville:
I still have these cups, that I was telling you about. I wanted to drop them off to you for your restaurant. Can I drop it off to you today?
Text message received from Jayville:
Around what time? I'm not free til bout after 1
Text message sent to Jayville:
Okay, 2p
Text message received from Jayville:
Meet me at my house on the Northside
Text message sent to Jayville:
K, I don't have that address to send it to me
Text message received from Jayville:
K
***

I can't wait to see Jayville. It has only been two days since the last time I seen him, and he laid that dick down. Oh my gosh, I have been thinking about that night non-stop. It makes me realizes how boring my sex life was in my marriage. We really lacked intimacy and damn this is what I have been missing out on. I am so happy I got out when I did. Now I am trying to figure out what I want to wear to see Jayville. I want to look very sexy when I see him. I am going to put this black all-purpose sweater dress on with my black stilettos. I took my braids out last night, so he will see my beautiful long natural hair. I was never blessed with the face to wear different crazy colors, wigs, lace front, weave, and look better with it. I look way better with my real hair versus weave.

***

Text message sent to Jayville:

I am here. Come outside.

As he opened the door to walk outside towards me, I instantly got butterflies in my stomach. I felt like a little kid with a crush. In that moment I realized he got me.

"Damn, you are looking good. I like your hair." Jayville said.

I unlocked my trunk so he can grab the cups and I opened my car door to walk towards the trunk where he was.

"Damn, you are looking so damn good. You can't be coming over here looking that damn good. Damn you are making me want to eat that pussy." Jayville expressed.

"Oh really, Bahahaha" I laughed.

"Yes, you are making me want to eat that. You coming inside?" He asked.

I nodded my head yes, but I wanted to scream Hell Yes! That was my first time at this house that he referred to as his Northside house. It was a lot smaller than his main house, but it was fully furnished. I sat down and waited while he put the cups up that I gave him in his back storage.

"So, what you got going on today?" he asked me.

"I need a plug in one of my tires. When I leave here, I plan of stopping by a tire place." I told him.

"Ohok" he responded.

As he came closer to me and approached me. I noticed he

got down on his knees in front of me, while I was sitting on the couch. He spread my legs apart and scooted me down and started sucking and licking the sins out of my kitty cat. I wanted to scream but just kept my moaning in moderation. I was nutting all in his mouth and I can tell he didn't mind because every time I nutted, he would moan and slurp up my kitty cat juice. I was passed cloud nine, at this point I needed him inside of me. I signaled him to get up so I can feel his penetration. He got up, went and grabbed a condom. When he came back, he slid his pants down brushed me against the wall and turned me around to face the wall and slid his penis in from the back. It felt so damn good, I couldn't control myself at that point. I was screaming, moaning, and throwing it back. I was so happy I didn't wear any underwear with that dress because it was easy access for him to go right to work. I kept my dress on while we were having sex. I forgot to take it off. I guess we were both so caught up in the moment it didn't even matter that it was still on. He pulled out and lifted me in the air and started eating my kitty kat again with me upside down in the air. This shit is feeling so great, I feel lost in his world.

"Damn, baby! Let me get you a washcloth." Jayville suggested.

As we finished having the best extended quickie ever in life. When he came back with the washcloth, I grabbed it and went into his guest bathroom. Damn, I just realized that I didn't even get a tour of this house. We just went straight to the business and time was going by so fast. I still needed to get my tire plunged and pick Kai up from daycare.

"Please, don't come over here anymore looking that damn

good." Jayville suggested again while smiling.

"ha-ha" I laughed.

"I have to go and get this tire fix." I reminded him.

I then noticed he reached into his pocket and pulled out a bank roll of money. He started counting and gave me some of it.

"Here, this is for your tire and some gas." He told me as he handed me the cash.

He then walked me to my car and opened my car door. We kissed and I went on my way. I am feeling so sprung already I can't even think about what just happened right now. I have to much going on right now I must save our interaction as a mental note, and I will reflect on it later.

***

Finally, home from running all my errands.

Text message received from Jayville:

Wyd

Text message sent to Jayville:

Just got finish bathing Kai

Text message received from Jayville:

I been thinking about you all day

Text message sent to Jayville:

Oh yea, what you been thinking about?

Text message received from Jayville:

You are so amazing. I don't see how any man could let you go. You are like the perfect girl.

Text message sent to Jayville:

Text message received from Jayville:

Frfr how is your business coming along?

Text message sent to Jayville:

Its coming along.
Text message received from Jayville:
Did you order your flyers and business cards yet?
Text message sent to Jayville:
Not yet. I'm going to do it later this week
Text message received from Jayville:
Can I call you
Text message sent to Jayville:
Yes
"Hello" I answered the incoming call from Jayville
"Yes, I was thinking that you should start writing out your goals for your business. Write out top 3 things you want to accomplish for each week." He explained
"Yes, that's true." I replied
"Make sure you order those business cards and flyers. That's important to have." He suggested.
"Okay, I will" I told him.
"Have you considered being a financial consultant? Like doing tax preparation?" he asked.
"I haven't, a lot of people always suggest that I do tax preparation. But I am just not into the financial portion like that." I explained.
"You can make a lot of good money from doing that. What about insurance, owning your own insurance agency?"
"Its funny that you mentioned that, because I am interested in that. I wouldn't mind doing that. I plan to look more into financial consulting too though." I told him.
"Yes, I think you would be great at it. It would be a great added piece to your business and what your doing now already." He suggested.
"So, what's new with the building you put a bid in for? Any

updates?" I asked him.

"Yes, I forgot to tell you earlier before I was distracted by that fine ass! I am closing on it real soon." He answered.

"That is so dope! I am so happy for you!" I told him.

"Thanks, I'm planning to go to China for two weeks next month and I have to start renovation and construction on that property. It's going to be a lot of work" he responded.

"Your going to China in two weeks, that so cool!" I responded.

"Oh yes, damn I thought I mentioned it to you. Yes, this my second time going. I went two years ago. I am going for two weeks with my cousin. Man, you can find everything over there for dirt cheap. It's amazing." He explained.

"I wish I could go with you and your going to be gone for a long time. We should plan a trip somewhere; I love to travel too" I suggested.

"Yes, we can its up to you. Just let me know" He responded.

"So, how is the food in China?" I asked.

"The food isn't the greatest, I still eat at American restaurants when I am there. It is beautiful though." He answered.

"I could only imagine. I am going to miss you while you are gone. Is your phone still going to work while you are there?" I asked.

"Yes, it will still work. I got T-Mobile Baby, it works everywhere. Ha-ha" he laughed.

"Well, I could image that Sprint doesn't, but I am not one hundred percent sure." I responded.

We talked for about an hour more about everything. I was still feeling kind of sad knowing that he was going to be

leaving within the next 30-45 days. I just didn't know what to expect once he is away. I don't even know if he is even talking another woman. I know he mentioned his cousins are going with him but how true is that really. Now I am feeling this jealous and insecure spirit come over me.
***

Two weeks went by and me and Jayville are still going strong in our friendship. We have been spending a lot of time together. I have been seeing him at least twice a week during his busy schedule. We take turns texting each other the "Good morning text" every morning.

"Hi Babe" I answered to Jayville's incoming call

"What are you doing this morning?" he asked.

"Nothing I am just getting up." I told him.

"Let's go to breakfast. How long will it take you to get ready?" he asked.

"It should take me about an hour to get ready and thirty minutes to get to you. I would say about two hours." I responded.

"Try to make it one hour, ha-ha" he said

"I'll try!" I responded.

"Alright" he said before hanging up.

Damn, now I must figure out what I am going to wear and ask my Mom to watch Kai again. I hate to ask her again and keep her in my business with him. It really sucks that me and Bama aren't on speaking terms right now. I can't wait for him to come around so he can get Kai sometimes. I don't even want to think about that situation right now. Jayville is keeling me grounded, motivated, and my mind off my divorce. Especially off Bama dead beat ass.
***

One and a half hour later I pulled up to Jayville's main

house. I was so excited to him. He is my Baby! I never thought I would ever love again or fall again but he just caught me by surprise.

Text message sent to Jayville:

I'm outside Babe

Text message received from Jayville:

K come inside

I grabbed my purse and got out of the car. Before I can ring the doorbell, he came to the door.

"You look nice" he expressed to me as he hugged and kissed me.

"Thanks Daddy, you're not ready to go. I am hungry." I told him.

"Yes, we can leave." He answered.

"Where are we going to go? I love I-HOP" I suggested.

"Oh okay, I was going to take you to Cracker Barrel. But if you want to go there, we can." He replied.

"Yes, let's do I-Hop" I responded excited.

***

We had such a great breakfast at IHOP. We went back to his house and spent most of the rest of the day together before I decided to leave.

Text message received from Bestie Punkin:

Bitch, u good?

Text message sent to Bestie Punkin:

Sis!!!!! Yes, OMG I have to catch you up. I'm about to call you. This is too much to text.

"Hello" Punkin answered.

"Sis!!!!" I responded.

"I haven't heard from you in about a month. Are you okay?' She asked concerned.

"I'm grreeaaaatttt!" I answered

"So, catch me up. We really haven't talked like that since your divorce. I was giving you, your time and space but damn a whole month." She responded.

"I am sorry Hun, but remember I told you about Jayville?" I reminded her.

"Yes, the good catch. What about him?" She asked.

"Sis! We have been spending so much time together. I am falling for him. I feel like I love him." I told her.

"Are you sure its love?" She asked.

"Yessss, I love him Sis!" I assured her.

"I don't think you love him, yo ass just sprung" she said.

"So, you think its just lust?" I asked.

"Yes, I do" She answered.

"No, its not lust though, I really feel like I love him. The connection I have with him is so strong. I feel like I am connected to him and like we been knew each other. He is everything I ever wanted in a man. I love his drive, how he motivates and pushes me. It is more to him than our bomb ass sex. He is more of a man than Bama could've ever been. I mean he is just different, and I love the way he looks at me Sissss!!"

"Okay now, I hear you! I believe you and can't wait to meet him" She said.

"Me too Sis, I just left him. We spent the whole day together." I told her.

"Have you talked to Bama?" She asked.

"Girl, I haven't talked to him and I am not going to reach out to him. It is just sad that Kai is getting mistreatment and its even sadder that I have to pass by his apartment everyday to take Kai to school." I told her.

"Damn, that's hard Sis. You are strong." She responded.

"Jayville is helping me as well with taking my mind of it.

Girl, I even cried on the phone with him about it." I told her.

"Really? Be careful with that too though. You don't want him to think you still want Bama ass" She suggested.

"You are so right. I am so over Bama. I don't want him at all. I hope he isn't thinking that way. You know my ass is so emotional and it does bother me that he walked away treating me like we didn't just spend all those years together." I told her.

"Girl, I am surprised he let a good woman like you go Sis. Like I can't believe it." She explained.

"Sis, I just got to Kai school. I am going to hit you later." I told her.

"Okay, Boo! Love you!" She said.

"Love you too" I replied

I've been knowing Punkin for over a decade. We went to high school together. Its so funny because we were kind of like enemies in high school because we both dated the same guy at the same time. Once we both stopped messing with him and compared notes on it all we have been inseparable. She is like a sister to me. Of course, we don't get along all the time, but we always put our egos aside and talk it out. I love my bestie, but I had to get off the phone with her because I don't feel like reflecting on how Bama isn't shit. I guess I am still suppressing the pain.

***

Text message received from Jayville:
Good morning Gorgeous
Text message sent to Jayville:
Good morning Handsome
Text message received from Jayville:
How are you doing?

Text message sent to Jayville:
I am doing okay. I was thinking we should plan a trip to Cuba in July. Since both of our birthday around that time period. What do you think?
Text message received from Jayville:
That cool. Why Cuba though?
Text message sent to Jayville:
Because you never been to Cuba, I want to go somewhere we both haven't been. I heard Cuba was dope.
Text message received from Jayville:
LOL. Okay just let me know the dates you wana go.
Text message sent to Jayville:

K, Papi. I can't believe you leaving next week for China ☹
Text message received from Jayville:
IKR. I am dreading this long ass flight. I am going to need some pills for this trip.
Text message sent to Jayville:
Aww I could only imagine. I miss you already!
Text message received from Jayville:
I miss you too
***

Me and Jayville haven't missed a day without speaking and I am so attached. I am so excited our trip is booked for Cuba and its two months away. I am counting down already. It is something to look forward too. Our first international trip together. I wish he wasn't leaving for China tomorrow. I am glad that he is leaving, so he can hurry back.
Text message received from Jayville:
Wyd
Text message sent to Jayville:

I am waiting on you.

Text message received from Jayville:

Okay, come to Northside house. You on the way now.

Text message sent to Jayville:

Yes, Papi. I'll be there in 30minutes.

***

"Babe, are you going to miss me?" I asked Jayville as we embraced each other with a hug and a kiss.

"Of course, what kind of question is that." He responded. We spent the next three hours together, but I knew and can tell he was tired. I didn't want to keep him any much longer and I needed to get back home. Being that I am still living with my Mom I am mindful of the hours I come home. I don't want her in my business with Jayville. It was so hard to leave him because I am so attached. I wonder if he is attached like me.

***

My Baby is in China. We have been talking everyday since he has been there. I have been productive since he has been away in China. I got a job offer back into Corporate America. I will be back to work in two weeks, and I found an apartment that I was approved for. I am planning to move into my apartment after our trip to Cuba. It is like literally one week after we come back. I don't know what I was thinking and didn't realize how close the dates were. I am really wondering if the dynamics of me and Jayville relationship will change when I get back to work. Right now, everything is so spontaneous with us. We go to the movies in the daytime and spend a lot of time during the day when my son is in daycare. We rarely spend time together at night. I don't know why I am feeling weird about it but for some reason I am. I talk to him about my son and he asks about him, but we still haven't discussed him meeting my son. That is something that I am not comfortable with anytime soon. I know if we do become exclusive than he must meet Kai. I just want to make sure we have a solid foundation before I bring my son in the mix. Kai's Dad is a big enough disappointment right now. Even though I am smitten over Jayville there are still things I am questioning myself. I still haven't met any of his family and I only seen one friend. I am beginning to question where I stand with him and in his life. Then I think about his actions and I am like, well we do speak every day. He does take me out on dates, and he is really engaged with me. I am taking each day one step and day at a time. We will see hoe everything plays out after our trip and I move into my own place.

***

Text message received from Bestie Punkin:
What u up to?
Text message sent to Bestie Punkin:
I am okay. Ready to see Jayville. He'll be here tonight.
Text message received from Bestie Punkin:
Oh Shit, I know you can't wait
Text message sent to Bestie Punkin:
SIS!! OMG I CAN'T! LOL
Text message received from Bestie Punkin:
LMFAO

***

Text message received from Jayville:
Good morning Sexy
Text message sent to Jayville:
Good morning Baby
Text message received from Jayville:

Try to be here by 1p so we can catch this 2pm movie.
Text message sent to Jayville:
K, Baby
***

Two hours later, I am pulling up to Jayville's main house. His screen door was already opened. I decided to stay in the car since he was able to see that I pulled up. He came out his door talking on one of his cell phones. He opened the car door gave me a hug and a kiss and signaled that he was on an important call. I just started driving. It was raining so bad, it just started pouring down out of nowhere the further I was driving. We finally pulled up at the movies and we just parked because the rain was so bad. We weren't even sure if we wanted to get out the car.

"So, what you want to do?" He asked me.

"I am not trying to get my hair wet." I told him.

"Bahahaha" he laughed.

Then there was an awkward pause between us.

"What's going on with you? What's wrong?" he asked me. He was able to connect with me and tell that I needed to tell him something.

"I don't know how to tell you." I told him.

"Tell me what? Just say it." He responded.

"I don't know if I want to" I said.

"Your period late?" he asked.

"Damn, how did you know? Its two days late" I told him.

"See that's why I always use condoms, and you saying you don't like condoms. This why I shouldn't listen to that. Let's go!" he said.

"Let's go where?" I asked.

"To get a pregnancy test. There is a CVS in that plaza at the next light" He said.

"Okay, I am not saying that I am pregnant. I am just saying that I am two days late." I explained.

"I knew it was weird you didn't mention anything about your period." He told me.

I'm thinking in my head damn he has been keeping up with my periods. When we pulled up to the CVS, he gave me all the money that was in his pocket. I didn't even count it I just grabbed the roll of money and stuffed it in my person. I was trying to prevent from crying. Our day went downhill that fast. I really wasn't sure if I was pregnant or not, but I do have irregular periods from time to time. I went and brought 4 pregnancy tests. I got back in the car and gave him the bag with the pregnancy tests in them.

"I thought you were intune with your body." He said.

"I am intune with my body." I explained.

"Naw, you can't be. Let's go back to the house so you can take these test" he said.

"Babe, I don't think I am pregnant" I told him again.

"We will see soon. That's why you in here playing, Confessions by Usher?" he asked me and then started laughing.

I couldn't help but laugh too because it helped change the mood and ease the tension in the air.

"No, that isn't why." I responded to him.

We pulled back up to his house. When we entered the house, I went straight into his master bathroom to take the test. I am so nervous right now. All I keep thinking is, I just divorced… I just divorced… this cant be happening right now. What are you showing and telling me God? I finally opened one of the pregnancy boxes up and took the test.

Results= Negative-Not pregnant.

What a sigh of relieve. I am opened the second pregnancy test box. Results= Negative-Not pregnant.

I was so ecstatic at that point and felt like I proven my point to be right the entire time. Jayville came into his room as I was walking out the bathroom. I smiled at him.

"I'm not pregnant! I told you I wasn't" I told him excited.

"You weren't sure either, you were scared too. Stop fronting" He responded.

"Hahaha, no I wasn't." I replied.

"Yes, you were. I can't believe you not intune with your body." He expressed again.

I am trying to figure out why he keeps accusing me of not being intune with my body. Like its starting to irritate me at this point.

"So, its stop raining do you want to go back to the movies?" I asked him.

"I really prefer to go to the movies earlier in the day when it's not crowded. If you want to go, we can go." he replied.

"Yes, I really do want to see this new Avenger movie. I waited for you to get back from China to see it." I explained.

"Okay, let so back up there then. I do want to see it too." He expressed.

We got back in my car and I drove back up there. I must admit the energy was still off between us and I don't know what he was thinking. I just felt like in this very moment this was going to make us or break us. It kind of scared me. We pulled back up to the movies and it was more crowded than it was when we first came up there.

"They are saying that all the shows are booked up until tonight." Jayville told me.

"Damn, it seems like it's not meant for us to see this

movie." I told him.

"Yes, what you wana do?" he asked me.

"Id rather just go back to your spot" I told him.

"Okay, lets go!" He said.

When we pulled back up to his spot I was debating if I even wanted to get out the car or if I want to go home. The energy was still off but I still wanted to talk more. I just believe in clearing out the energy with people that you care about before you leave them. In this situation I am going to just stick around for about an hour before I go home to get a feel of where his head is it.

***

Two days later and I feel still feel a little dent in our situationship. We are still talking and texting, but it still feels a little off for some reason. I am taking it one day at a time and keeping positive thoughts.

"Hey Bestie" I answered.

"What you up to?" She asked.

"Girl, I was going to call you. I don't know its been a lil off with Jayville since the pregnancy scare. Like we not texting as much anymore." I told her.

"That nigga done had a surreal moment and a reality check. That's what the fuck happened Sis." She explained.

"Damn, I didn't even look at it that way." I told her.

"You guys are moving pretty fast, and that shit hit him. Yall need to be using protection anyway. Girl you can't trust no Nigga enough like that with your life. You don't even know him well enough. What if you would've been pregnant and he got ghost on you. Then what? You should be happy as hell right now and not sad. You just divorced. You shouldn't even be trying to be back in another commitment." She explained.

"Oh my gosh, you just said a mouthful right now. Like you are so right. I just feel like he is the one, but you are so right!" I agreed.

'Girl, yes! How he is behaving now is his true self. You better pay attention to the signs." She warned me.

"Your so right. So how are you and your Boo? Yall good?" I asked her.

"Yes, we good. I just don't trust his ass but we good. Ha-ha" she laughed.

"ha-ha, girl we can't trust none of them!" I laughed.

"Well, ima let you go Boo. You know I don't like talking on the phone like that. Just checking on you!" She responded.

"Yes, I know. Ill text you later. Love u!" I told her.

"Love you too Boo" she replied.

***

One month later and it is Cancer season. Jayville birthday is today. I am taking him out to breakfast. We haven't been seeing each other as much as we use too. He has been so focused on his new business venture and I am back to work. I haven't seen him in two weeks. I was really looking forward to his fine ass, but we couldn't do anything sexual because my period was on. I was so depressed that it decided to come on during this moment. I will never question God, so everything happens for a reason. I pulled up to the restaurant and he was already sitting inside waiting on me. As soon as I walked in, I was able to spot him. I went right over to him. He stood up and greeted me and somehow as he was complimenting me, he wastes his drink all over his shirt and table.

"Damn, you look so fucking good. You are stopping traffic." He told me.

He always had a way of flattering me and I never felt as if he was just trying to fill my head up. I believe every word he tells me because he always looks into my eyes when he compliments me. Its something about the way he looks and gaze into my eyes. I feel lost in the moment. The connection is so strong for me. We ate at the restaurant and then he wanted to take me back by the renovated event center. I followed him over there. When we arrived, I was so impressed with the results. It looked so nice from the outside to end. I had an immediate flashback of when he first brought me by the location before it, he even purchased it. I was beyond proud of the finished results. He dimmed the lights and started playing music. He grabbed me close to him and we started slow dancing. He then turned me around and I started grinding on him to the beat. He lifted my dress up and at that moment I was slippery wet wishing my cycle wasn't on. I had to signal him nicely.

"Baby, I'm code red" I told him.

"Damn" he said.

He pulled my dress back down and we started back kissing. I am quite sure I wanted to more than he did. Kissing makes me so horny, he makes me so horny! We chilled for about another hour at his event center. Until, I had to leave. I wanted to hit the shopping outlets to continue to shop for our trip. It was only fourteen days away and being that I am back to work I only have the weekends.

Text message sent to Jayville:

Baby, I miss you already.

Text message received from Jayville:

Make sure you get some short sets, and swimming shoes.

Text message sent to Jayville:

Okay, Daddy

I am beyond excited about our first trip. My mom thinks it's still too early for us to be traveling together. I mean it has been six months now and we talk every single day. I felt connected and safe around him from our first encounter and he did take me to Orlando on our first date. If he wanted to kidnap me, I am quite sure he would've did it then. This trip will either make or break us. Lord knows after the year I just had. I need a trip out of the country more than anyone. I am counting down.
***

It's my Birthday! I am so excited. This is the first birthday I celebrated in years as a single woman, I am Divorced! No Bama! I am so happy about life right now. I know Jayville is supposed to take me to out to eat later. My auntie is coming over and there is supposed to be a Caribbean day party that I want to stop by before I meet up with Jayville.
***

"Haapppppyyyyy Birtttthhhdddaaaayyyy to yooooouuuu" Jayville sang in the phone.

"ha-ha, thanks Babe" I replied blushing through the phone.

"What are you doing?" He asked.

"I am waiting for my Auntie to get over here, so we can eat this cake my Mom got me. I am thinking about hitting up this day party." I told him.

"Day party, what day party?" He asked.

"It is a Caribbean day party it starts around 2p." I answered.

"My Sister host day parties. Her name Nikki, you going to Nikki day party?" He asked.

"Naw, I doubt its her party. This is a Caribbean day party."

I suggested.

"Well, how you trying to go to a day party, and I am trying to take you out to eat and I wanted to catch this movie too." He said.

"I didn't know you were trying to link up early. I thought you wanted to link up later this evening." I told him.

"Yea, I wanted to catch this movie. Just let me know what you trying to do." He replied before hanging up.

Jayville energy was a little off which surprised me. I never question the things he does and it's my birthday on top of it. He needs a chill pill.

Text messaged received from Jayville:

Don't worry about it. Go to the day party and have fun

Text messaged sent to Jayville:

I still want to see you. I was going to swing by the day party first

Text messaged received from Jayville:

Nah, we can go another time.

Text messaged sent to Jayville:

No, I want to see you today. Its my birthday and I want to spend it with you.

Text messaged received from Jayville:

Okay, come now

Text messaged sent to Jayville:

K, give me hour

My auntie just arrived. Now I am trying to figure out how I am going to get ready within an hour and still spend time with my family. I never seen this selfish side of Jayville before, but I still want to be with him. I never seen this controlling side of him or maybe I have been blind to it the entire time. I have knots in my stomach now and this is not a good feeling for me. I just got out of a bad marriage and I don't want to relive that feeling. We still aren't exclusive or in a committed relationship. I just don't want to feel like I am allowing him to have control over me when he is not officially my Man.

***

I just pulled up to Jayville house an hour late. There is no way I could've just rushed out on my birthday and not spent time with my Auntie. I still felt bad for leaving when I did. I know that me and Jayville have this trip next week to Cuba. I want us to get along before the trip. It would suck if we are odds trying to travel together and besides it my Birthday. I want some Birthday sex on top of that.

"Hey Babe, sorry I'm late" I told Jayville as I embraced him with a hug and a kiss.

"You lucky it's your birthday, Ima let that slide, ha-ha" he laughed.

He looked happy and excited to see me. To think I was worried about how his energy would have been when I arrived. I guess I assume a lot and over think.

"You look nice." He told me.

"Thanks Babe and you're not even dressed to go out" I replied.

"I was waiting for you to get here. I'm getting dressed now but before I do bring that ass here." He said.

He grabbed me closer to him, sticked his tongue down my throat while grabbing my right butt cheek.

"You still want to go out to eat or you want this dick now?" He asked me.

"I am hungry Babe, I still want to eat." I told him.

I am thinking to myself, it is still my birthday Nigga. You about to spend some money on me. I always get some of that dick.

"ha-ha, okay where you want to go eat at?" He asked me.
"Its up to you Babe, wherever you want to take me. I'll let you surprise me." I suggested.
"Okay, I'm going to get dressed now" he replied
This man had me rushing to get to him and he isn't even ready. This really kind of irritated me but I am not going to trip over it. He slick starting to sign me toxic sign behavior. I am still so happy to see him, so I am not going to much thought in his behavior today. I love spending time with him and being up under him. I feel so safe when I am with him. He just makes me feel in such an indescribable way that feels so good to the soul.
***

The day has finally arrived! I am beyond excited! Jayville should be here any minute now to pick me up. I feel like this trip will shape the direction of our relationship.
Text messaged received from Jayville:
I am outside.
Text messaged sent to Jayville:
K, I'm coming now.
I opened my door and he got out his car and walked towards me to grab my bag. He placed it in the car, and he seemed as if he was still tired.
"Babe, you still tired?" I asked.
"Yes, who the fuck book morning flights this early? Why did you book the flight so early? I never leave out this early." He responded.
"Babe, I sent you the itinerary months before this trip and you approved it." I told him.
"Yea, but I didn't read that shit and that was months ago." He explained.
"Well, you woke up and we here Babe." I told him.

"What is there even to do in Cuba? My homeboy went and said it wasn't shit to do. It just a lot of Cigar smoking and antique cars there to see. Isn't much exciting shit to do there." He said.

Now this is what I didn't want to happen. I didn't want to start this trip off bad energy. He got me questioning myself. I sent him the itinerary more than once and in advance. I am trying to figure out what is going on with him. I am going to tune out this behavior and remain positive. I am still excited to visit Cuba.

I am so excited we finally arrived in Cuba. As we walked out towards that exit there was a lady holding a sign with our names on it. We followed her. We both were expecting our car to be already there, and it wasn't. Here we go again with Jayville and his negative attitude.

"So, you mean to tell me that our transportation not even here? What the fuck." He said.

I took it upon myself to ask the lady the status of the transportation. She advised me that they are on there way. Unfortunately, I limo didn't pull up or a nice town car. A small cab pulled up.

"You can't be fucking serious?" Jayville said.

"Babe, I didn't know it would've been a small taxi. The hotel set this up." I told him.

"Yo ass aint planning no more trips going forward." He said sounding upset.

At this point I am praying the hotel is legit. I booked the entire trip, so I played it safe. I booked Hilton resort, an American hotel franchise. I didn't think the Hilton franchise could ever go wrong. When we got to the hotel, I was so happy it did look as good as I expected it too. I didn't find anything wrong with the hotel but of course

Jayville did. He complained about how basic the hotel was. He just couldn't understand how he paid thousands of dollars for this hotel. He started insulting me for the booking of the overall trip. He kept referencing to being an Experienced traveler and blah blah. I tried to remain positive because I never seen him carry so much negative energy before. Like, is this the real him that I am seeing right now. He is behaving like a straight asshole. In the beginning of this trip I was keeping it cool but now my positivity has turned into negativity. I can't even pretend anymore. I matched his energy and now I am pissed. We both were arguing at this point with each other. I don't even want to be in the same room with him. This trip has turned into a disaster. If I never knew anything else, I knew Jayville was a spoiled brat.

This trip isn't going good at all. He is complaining about everything from the food, pool, beach, activities. I remember hearing him at one point tell me that I lack common sense. I automatically just had a flashback of arguing with my ex. I have been there and done that with the back in forth insults. I am passed that now and don't want to revisit it. Not with him or anyone. I love him too much at this point to continue to argue with him.

This trip was a bad idea from the beginning to where we are now. I am withholding my tears of disappointment, not only in him but myself. Why is it so hard for him to enjoy me on this beautiful Island? I booked this trip for us to enjoy each other and for us to bond on a deeper level. It is obvious that isn't what he wants. So now I am confused, why did he agree and invested in this trip.

We are moving too fast. I just want to go home….

CHAPTER 5

GAMES

I am so happy to be back home with Kai. I am still feeling hurt and disappointed by that disastrous trip with Jayville. I haven't even revealed to Punkin how bad that trip was. It is too embarrassing. I only gave my Mom pieces because she felt my energy. The trip was so horrible we came back two days earlier. I still want to cry thinking about it.
***
Text messaged received from Jayville:
Good morning
Text messaged sent from Jayville:
Good morning
We haven't really talked since we been back from the trip. He does make sure to send me the "good morning" text every morning. Even if that is the only thing, he will say to me. It seems like I am the one dragging the conversations now with him. If I ask him a question, he will respond but other than that he isn't really talking to me. I am feeling so confused. Are we done? I am scared to ask him because I fear what the answer maybe. I really need to talk to Punkin. All my Mom keeps saying is I should of never went on the trip with him and blah blah. I really don't want to hear that because its too late at this point. I fell in love with this man and my heart is weak for him. The signs are present to walk away, and I am too scared too.
Text messaged sent to Bestie Punkin:
Are you busy? Please call me
"Hey Girl" I answered the incoming call from Punkin.
"You okay?" She asked.
"No… I'm not…." I whispered in the phone before I broke down crying.
"Sis, its okay. please calm down. Talk to me" Punkin said.
After two minutes of silence and I was able to put my

words together. I stopped crying.

"Jayville, like I don't know what I did wrong." I told her.

"You see this is what I feared. Sis, you don't need this right now. You just got out of a bad marriage. You shouldn't be crying ova nan Nigga." She advised me.

"I know it, but I fell in love with him. I feel so stupid right now. Its like that trip to Cuba ruined our relationship. He does still text me every morning, but sometimes that's all I get. I just want it to be like it was." I told her.

"You know they say sometime trips can make or break you. I rather you just let it go now and move on. I mean you are Single. He never gave you a commitment. So, Sis this nigga on games. Like he been playing with your mind and emotions from the jump." She suggested.

"You think this has been a joke to him?" I asked desperately.

"Yes, I do. He knew you just got divorced so I mean he just having fun. You said this man in his late 30s with no kids, never been married, he got money and shit. Man, this dude is an experienced Player. Sorry to say he aint who you think he is Sis. He really aint shit like the rest of these Niggas out here." She said.

"Damn, you just stung me Sis. Like I don't know what to say. I really need to just talk to him, but I am scarred too. I feel like I should've set that expectation with him from the beginning and I didn't." I responded.

"I know it hurts and I know you have feelings. You are beautiful, smart, independent. Like what do you really need him for? You need to be talking to at least 3-4 dudes at once Sis. Keep your options open! You just got out of a bad situation with Bama and I see firsthand how you were a good woman to him." she said.

"Yes, I hear everything you are saying but I mean this man has been there for me and supporting me. I've cried with him on the phone about my Bama. He has been my motivation and support system. So, it is not that easy for me to just walk away and say Fuck him! Like it's not. I just need to woman up and have this conversation with him. I will know where to go from there." I told her.

"I agree 100% with you and I support whatever decision you want to do. I am just saying as soon as a Nigga stop showing interest and shit start slowing down, changing up, there is someone else taking his time." Punkin said.

"I know that's the truth. I haven't seen him in almost a month. Girl I just realized I haven't seen him since the trip." I confessed.

"Well, damn what happened in Cuba? Like Sis, what really happened?" She asked.

"I wish I can tell you. It was like from the time he picked me up to go to the airport he had bad energy. He was also complaining about one of his tenants being late on they rent and playing games with him. He was so negative about everything. From the hotel, to the restaurant food. I mean everything was negative. We weren't even intimate like that on the trip. We had sex only once and that was the last night there. When I tell you that was the worst sex we ever had. It just felt forced on his end and it wasn't good. It was just a trip of disaster. It felt like the entire trip was cursed." I told her.

"Damn, Sis! That sounds so bad. I am so sorry you had to experience that. Girl, you good. I wouldn't even want to fuck with him again after that shit. Fuck no!" she said.

"That's what I am saying like he still communicating with me but its just not engaging. Its like he is barely holding on. I am just going to talk to him." I replied.

"Well, Sis I just don't want you to be blind or get hurt again." She suggested.

"I am already hurting again because I fell in love with him. I didn't even think this would be possible. I never thought I could love again after Bama. I never thought I could be stupid again. Jayville got my ass. UGH!!!" I yelled."

"It's okay Sis. Just talk to him." She suggested.

"Ookie dokie. I'll keep you updated." I told her.

"Okay, Boo!" She responded.

"Love you Chica! Thanks for your ear as always." I told her.

"Always, Love U!!!" Punkin yelled before hanging up.

***

Text messaged received from Jayville:

Good morning

Text messaged sent to Jayville:

Good morning, I need to talk to you.

Text messaged received from Jayville:

What's up

Text messaged sent to Jayville:

Can I call you now?

Text messaged received from Jayville:

Yea

"Heyyyy!" I yelled in the phone after he picked up.

"What's up?" He said.

"I feel like I haven't talked to you in forever. How is the event center going?" I asked.

"It is going great. I am booked up for the next three months." He responded.

"I am so happy and proud of you! I knew it was a great investment. I miss talking to you." I told him.

"I miss talking to you too." He responded.

"It just feels like you don't like me anymore. I haven't seen you in almost a month. I am not used to going this long without seeing you. It just feels weird." I said.

"Well you are working, and I been really busy too with this event center and my other businesses." He responded.

"I've been in my new place weeks now and you haven't been over here since." I mentioned to him.

"I tried to come over the first day you moved in and you shot me down. So, when I get some free time I will." He responded.

"Wowww! Really Jayville?" I asked him.

"What you mean?" He asked me.

"You are sounding like a real asshole right now. So, what's up with us? "Where do we stand?" I asked him aggressively.

"We still talk, everyday don't we?" he answered.

"I mean yes, you send me a "good morning" text every day. Somedays that is the only response I may get from you." I told him.

"To be honest. You just got a divorce. I am not about to be your rebound Nigga. You need this time to learn yourself, heal, and understand who you are. You are still mourning your divorce." He said.

"Wow, really?" I asked.

"Yes, you need to heal. You shouldn't even be trying to rush into a relationship and be on that lovey dub shit when you just divorced. Take this time to level up and focus on yourself. That why I haven't been hitting you up a lot. I want you to focus on leveling up and getting yourself together. You are seeming unstable and I want you to get stable." He said.

My heart dropped and my stomach was in knots. I didn't even know how to respond. I was fighting back tears and emotions. All I could do at this point was agree with him and get off the phone so I can cry my eyes out.

"Nigga, I fucking love you. I don't even think about my Ex-Husband. All I think about is you. I was healing within that marriage. But you know what!" I said, before he interrupted me.

"You can control love." He suggested.

"No, you cannot! That's insane for you to say that to me. I can't control that I fell in love with you!" I told him

"I am telling you, I control them feelings. I am focused on my money and business right now. The level up and that the mindset I am trying to teach you to be on." He said.

"You know what Jayville, now it all makes sense to me why the dynamic of our relationship changed. Thanks for your honesty. Well, ill talk to you later." I responded before hanging up.

I feel heartbroken right now. I can't even make sense out of what he was saying to me. Everything he said was indeed true but Daammmnnn. I am still confused on why he even spent so much time with me. Like why he invested the trips, dates, sex, money, etc. Now I am really feeling heartbroken.

***

"Hi Kai's Mother." My Mom said as I answered the phone.

"Hey Mom." I responded.

"What you been up to? How are you enjoying your new place" My Mom asked.

"I love it. I must admit it really hit me that I am a single Mom now. When I was living with you, I had the unlimited support and now I am here and it's just me." I told her.

"Aww, you still have us here for you. Don't feel like that." She expressed.

"Yes, I know. It's just now I am really facing the reality of my situation. It doesn't help that Bama hasn't been involved since the divorce. Its like he gave up on his son. That is the part that hurts the most. I just never would've imaged him being this kind of father ever." I explained.

"Well, sometimes it takes for situations like this to happen for people to reveal their true selves. I also know that he is still hurting too. He lost his family so just give him time too." She suggested.

"How much time do you think he is going to need Mom? Kai is getting older and he is missing the best years of Kai's life right now." I told her.

"Are you still a God-fearing woman?" She asked.

"Yes, I am!" I answered.

"You not acting like you are and you damn sure not sounding like one." She responded.

"You right Mom. I can't argue with that." I told her.

"So how does Jayville like your new place?" She asked.

"Ugh, he hasn't been over here yet" I answered.

"WHATTT! I can't believe it, why hasn't he?" She asked.

"I wish I can answer that. He wanted to come over the day I moved in, but I didn't let him because he didn't help me move. I was in my feelings. I didn't feel like it was fair for him to come over after all the hard work was done. So ever since then, he hasn't asked again. Honestly, I haven't seen him since Cuba. Its been a month now Mom." I told her.

"Baby, I am so sorry. I told you not to go on that trip with him. It was too soon for you. You just divorced. You spent to much time with him. I hope you haven't been sexually involved with him. Men like him have plenty of women that will do anything he want." She said.

"I could image. Well we talked and he suggested that I focus on myself. I mean we still do small talk here and there, but I guess our relationship is fading away." I suggested.

"Well, it maybe for the best. He is right, you do need to focus on you and Kai. A good man will come in time. Sound like he was just having fun and wasting time with you" She said.

"At first it didn't feel like that. I felt like it was real, genuine, and a soul connection. Now I am starting to feel like this has just been a game to him. I do know my worth Mom. I know that I am a great woman so I can't stress over it." I said

"You definitely shouldn't stress over it. I am still here when you need a break with Kai. Just let me know." She said.

"Thanks Mom." I said.

"No problem, I was just checking on you. One more thing, don't you ever allow another man to bring you back into a misery state of mind. Continue to chase your peace of mind." She said before hanging up the phone.

I must admit she was right. I didn't even realize how I began to loose myself. I started treating him and looking at him as if he was my man. He never made a commitment to me or even promised me a commitment. In this harsh reality I am rally hurting myself. He made it very clear to me that I just divorced, and I need to focus on healing. It is going to be hard but that is what I need to do.
***

Text messaged received from Jayville:
Wyd

Text messaged sent to Jayville:
Nothing, just finished bathing Kai
Text messaged received from Jayville:
K
Text messaged sent to Jayville:
So, am I ever going to see you again?
Text messaged received from Jayville:
Lol. Yea
Text messaged sent to Jayville:
It just doesn't seem like it. You haven't taken me out in a while
Text messaged received from Jayville:
When you wana go?
Text messaged sent to Jayville:
Wed
Text messaged received from Jayville:
K
***

Wednesday is here and I don't even know if I should go out to eat with him. Especially since I was the one that initiated it. Its been a month now and I am not understanding how he is okay with not seeing me. I am still in love with him, so I guess I might as well go.
Text messaged received from Jayville:
Wyd
Text messaged sent to Jayville:
I was just about to call you. What time you wana meet and where do you want to meet?
Text messaged received from Jayville:
Let's meet around 7p. I still don't know where yet because yo ass is picky and don't eat much of nothing.
Text messaged sent to Jayville:
LOL. Not true I eat the same stuff you eat just no meat, only fish.

Don't do me like that.
Text messaged received from Jayville:
Lol. Ill text you the address once I figure it out.
Text messaged sent to Jayville:
K Babe
***

I pulled up to the restaurant and noticed that his car wasn't in the parking lot.
Text messaged sent to Jayville:
Babe, I am here
Text messaged received from Jayville:
K get a table inside
Text messaged received from Jayville:
Ok
I got out the car and went in got a booth for us. This was a nice local restaurant. I never been here before, and I am hungry. I pray the food is good. Thank God here he comes in here looking so good. I love when he gets dressed and has clothes on, looking handsome.

He is always on the phone, always having tenant issues. I can't believe he walked to the table on the phone. This Man is so rude.

"Why you are looking at me like that?" He asked as he ended his phone call.

"That was rude. Why you didn't finish the call before you walked in here?" I asked him.

"I already had you waiting on me. If I would've stayed in the car then you would've been mad that I am late. Am I wrong?" He asked.

This is the issue I have with him. He always wants to be right. This Nigga right here is a real know it all. I am always right type a Nigga. I am a Boss, so I know everything and you know nothing. He is looking really good right now so let me just smile and enjoy this meal. I haven't seen him in forever already.

"Okay Babe, you are right" I told him.

"What's been going on with you? How is work and the business going?" He asked.

"Everything is going good." I answered.

"Your ex-husband, baby daddy aint been trying to come back in the picture?" he asked.

"What, No!" I answered.

"You know you only divorced him because you were mad. ha-ha" he laughed.

I felt so confused on where that comment came from. It was so random, and I am so lost right now.

"Ugh, No Jayville. When I divorced him, I was done with him. I was healing from him during the ending of our marriage. So, when I left him, I was done." I told him.

"Ohok, I hear yea" he responded.

"So, why haven't I seen you since Cuba?" I asked

"To be honest, I was mad ass hell at you, and I told myself I was giving you a break." He answered.

"What, why were you mad at me? What did I do?" I asked confused.

"Man, I left you in charge to plan the trip and you had enough time. You didn't plan a good trip, no itinerary, hotel was bad, food was bad. It just was a waste. I wasted 3K on that trip and we didn't even stay the entire time." he explained.

"Wow, I really didn't know it made that big of an impact on you." I answered.

"Do you want me to give you a stack back?" I asked.

"Nah, its not just about the money. It's just that I trust you

111

to handle everything. I travel a lot and been all over the world and never experience a trip like that. I took all kind of women on trips and I never spent that much money either." He said.

"We need a do over and you can plan the next trip." I told him.

All I could do id shake my head. Who is this man? This not the same man I fell in love with him. He is totally different now. Our conversation isn't even the same. I'm questioning why I even asked for this date. This situationship is over in his eyes I see by listening to things he was saying.

One hour later, as we were trying to leave out the rain poured down heavy. We didn't have an umbrella, so we went back into the restaurant for about fifteen minutes before it calmed back down. I can tell he was happy to see me, but it just seems like he has moved on to the next chick. I didn't hold his interest anymore. I just don't feel like he would be honest enough about our status. I am just going to continue to focus my son and myself.
***

Text messaged received from Jayville:
Good morning
Text messaged sent to Jayville:
Good morning Handsome
Text messaged sent to Jayville:
How is your day going?
Text messaged received from Jayville:
Good
Text messaged sent to Jayville:
I miss you
***

Text messaged received from Jayville:
Good morning
Text messaged sent to Jayville:
Good morning Babe
Text messaged sent to Jayville:
I want to see you
Text messaged received from Jayville:
Well see
Text messaged sent to Jayville:
I love you
***

Text messaged received from Jayville:
Good morning
Text messaged sent to Jayville:
Good morning
Text messaged received from Jayville:
wyd
Text messaged sent to Jayville:
Nothing u?
***

Text messaged received from Jayville:
Good morning
Text messaged sent to Jayville:
Good morning
Text messaged sent to Jayville:
How are you? I feel like you have no time for me. We barely talk now. You don't even be responding to me.
Text messaged received from Jayville:
Here you go always in your feeling
Text messaged sent to Jayville:
How? Im just saying. You barely respond to me. This is honesty
Text messaged received from Jayville:

I have a lot going on. I don't have time to be texting all day and sitting by my phone. I text you every day, don't I?
Text messaged sent to Jayville:
WOW! Good night
Text messaged received from Jayville:
Nite
This man has been a real-life asshole to me. I am hurting myself continuing to allow this to go on. This is pointless, we went from talking a lot, dates, trips to this. I don't even know what I am holding onto anymore. This man has done a 180-degree flip on me. Damn, I just thought he was different. Seems like he was just on games, just like every other Man out here. I was just too blind to see it.

CHAPTER 6

FACING MYSELF

I have been escaping and suppressing my emotions for months now. I feel so embarrassed to admit that to myself. I go from being a wife to another man's secret. I am facing another heart break, and this feels like a double attack on my heart. I don't understand how I even allowed myself to be so vulnerable to be led into this situation. I went through so much with Bama and yet I let another man come and play me again. The even sadder part is I still love this man and still have hope. I do understand that right now I need to fix myself. I need a life coach. I found two on Google that I am planning to contact. May the best life coach get hired. I need to make this investment in myself. I must understand why I keep getting myself in these miserable stuck situations with men.

***

I hired life coach Mike yesterday and we have our first session today via phone. I am a little nervous. I need to speak with someone who wont judge me and will genuinely help me identify my weak areas.

"Hi Mike!" I answered the incoming call.

"Hello! How are you doing today?" Mike asked.

"I am doing okay, u?" I asked.

"Well, well. I am so happy to partner with you. You did mention during the consultation that the first thing you want to tackle is self-discovery. You want to understand why you keep making bad decisions. Is that still correct?" He asked.

"Yes, it is still correct. I need your help to diagnose why I am like this" I suggested.

"Yes, I can help with that. I remember you telling me that you recently got divorced." He asked.

"Yes, that is true." I replied.

"Please, walk me through that marriage. Not during the courting phase. Walk me through the moment you both said, "I do" to the best of your ability." He said.

"We got married at the courthouse. We were supposed to have a destination wedding in Jamaica because that's where my family is from and my Dad lived. Being that his family was scared to travel overseas and couldn't really afford to make that trip we called it off. We both mutually decided that it's about us. At that time, I didn't care about having a wedding. I always felt like weddings were for the family members and others. On that day when we recited the vows its like part of me felt like we weren't ready. The look that was in his eyes on that day was so genuine, real, compassionate. The look he gave me took away of anxiety, fear, and self-doubt." I told the Life Coach.

"So, on your wedding day you felt like you weren't ready until you see the compassion in his eyes?" He asked.

"Yes, that is correct. Its like part of me knew I shouldn't be getting married to him right now because he wasn't ready. Then I seen the love in his eyes for me." I told him.

"Okay, I see. So, how was the first three months as newlyweds?" he asked.

"The first three months was surreal. I couldn't believe we were really married. I knew we were married because we did have the marriage license and the wedding certificate. It is just harder to believe when you don't have a wedding. I started realizing how important a wedding really is and I regretted not having one. We also said that we would renewal our vows at five years and have a ceremony. Its funny how life works because we divorced at year five. I am trying not to get emotional." I told the Life Coach

"I see there is still pain there. How are you dealing with

that pain from your divorce?" he asked.

"Honestly, I have just been suppressing it. Right after I divorced, I started dating someone, who I believed was my soul mate." I said before my Life Coach interrupted me.

"Okay, we aren't going to introduce that person right now. I want you to continue to focus and walk me through your marriage before the divorce. Please continue to walk me through the first three months" He demanded.

"Okay, so the first three months was great. Our level of intimacy was good, our finances was great, our communication was great. I was doing my duties as his wife. I was cooking, cleaning, being his everything." I told him.

"What I am hearing is, the first three months went well for you guys. There was a solid foundation within the first three months. You two were getting along, having sex, talking and you were playing your part as a domestic wife." He summarized in his words.

"Yes, I agree." I told him.

"Now walk me through the first year of marriage?" he asked.

"Whew! The first year was the roughest year for us. Yes, the first three months were great. Everything started going down hill after that." I told him.

"When you say downhill, please elaborate?" he asked.

"No disrespect Mike but I don't want to re live that marriage. I don't wish to continue to talk about it." I told him.

"Okay, if you don't want to talk about it or elaborate more, I do understand." He replied.

"Thank you" I responded.

"Talk to me about your father. How is your relationship

with your father?" he asked me.

"My father passed away two years ago of Cancer." I told him.

"I am so sorry to hear that" He responded.

"Its okay!" I suggested.

"Are you comfortable with talking about your Dad right now?" He asked.

"Yes, I am in a better space now. I can speak about him." I told him.

"That is good to hear. Please tell me more about your Father and how your relationship with him was." He asked again.

"This is a hard topic to discuss for me. My relationship with my Dad was rocky and unsteady. I remember from the age of eleven to eighteen I would visit my Dad was once a year. It was either in the summer or winter. He lived up North, so I enjoyed the winter visits to experience the snow." I said.

"Okay, so your father wasn't in the household or around daily? You would just spend time with him once a year. How long were those visits usually?" he asked.

"Yes, that is correct it would be once a year visits for about one or two weeks. I remember one time I did stay almost three weeks." I answered.

"Could you talk to me more about how those visits went? Did you guys do a lot of bonding during those visits?" He asked.

"I remember always being so excited to see my Dad. Then when I would get there, I would be ready to go sometimes. I was never able to spend the quality time with him like I wanted. He was always busy. I spent majority of the time there with my Stepmom and her son. The little time we spent together would be car rides. I remember the last time that I went there during the Christmas vacation, I was around twenty-two years old. That was my first time there in like two years and it ended up being my last time there. I surprised my Dad with a visit. He was so happy that I came to see him and spent Christmas and New years with him. That was the one time we really spent Daddy, daughter time together. I remember I chilled with him in his man cave for hours. We just talked and watched movies together. That is a good memory that I will forever cherish that I shared with my Father." I expressed as tears rolled down my face.

"I am happy to hear that you have great moments that you cherish and can hold onto. Describe to me the unsteady and rocky moments between you two?" he asked.

"My Dad didn't enter into my life until I was eleven years old. He missed out the important years to me. My Dad has never taken me to school or helped me with my homework. He never had a conversation with me about boys. He just didn't have an impact as a father should have. Yes, he did step up and take care of my Mother financially for me until I was 18. Then after I turned 18 it seemed like I had to pull teeth to get anything from him. He always gave me such a hard fight. We would talk on and off a lot. I remember one time I went almost 2 years without talking him." I shared.

"Really, why was it almost two years?" He asked.

"He cursed me out really bad when I was trying to express to him how I felt. When I was trying to clear the air and let him know how I felt about him and his relationship with me. He wasn't receptive to what I was saying. He went off on me and cursed me out as if I was a Bitch on the streets."

I explained.

"So, how were you able to rekindle your relationship after that?" he asked.

"I got a call from my brother Marvin, that he had cancer and he was in the hospital preparing for surgery. I needed to fly down to Jamaica when I can. During that time, I was pregnant with my son. I was in the second trimester. I instantly booked the next flight and went down to see him. Everything he said to me didn't even matter. I wasn't ready for him to leave this world. I still needed him here. Rather we were on good terms or bad terms." I clarified.

"That was really strong of you." He suggested.

"Yes, but then once the cancer was removed, and everything got back to normal with him. Just to provide you with an overview. We ended up clashing again. This time I just went months without talking to him. He did apologize and from there it was like our relationship was on and off up until he died. The cancer did come back in his system two years after it was removed because he didn't do the chemotherapy. I was there in Jamaica during his last stages. He died two days after I left him. Even after he died, I still feel like there was more I needed from him that I didn't get. I still felt empty and hurt." I told him.

"Why do you feel like you still felt empty and hurt?" He asked.

"It just felt like my Dad was still mad at me before he passed away. I couldn't shake that feeling. He was been dead now for two years. The first year I fought depression bad because I had no support dealing with the grieving period of his death. Bama, at the time didn't make the situation any better. He always brought up my short comings with my Father when I would mourn. He wasn't a good support system. I just felt so alone. It was such a hard time for me." I told him as tears ran uncontrollably down my face.

I decided to the end the life coaching session there. I knew this would've been hard, but I didn't realize how much pain I have been carrying around. My Dad never showed me love and I always waited around for him to make up for the years and he was just never able to fulfill. I never wanted to or could accept him for him. I was still and always hoping for more. This explains why I stick around and tolerate bullshit instead of walking away. At that moment I realized that I have Daddy issues that I need to heal from.

***

Text message received from Jayville:

Good morning

Text message sent from Jayville:

Good morning

I don't even understand why he is even still texting me every morning, or what we are doing. He still hasn't been my new place and it has been three months. This breaks my heart so much. Every time I ask him if he ever going to come, he keeps saying that he is. I guess its my fault for continuing to go to him and not demanding that he comes here. I shouldn't have to force someone to do something. A man will always make time to do what they want. I am just feeling like cutting this Nigga off and moving on with my life. At least this is what my mind is saying and telling me to do. My freaking heart is so blind and dumb. My heart won't allow me to move on from Jayville. He won my heart over. I have attachment issues that my Life coach has made it clear of.

Text message sent to Jayville:

It just seems like you aren't interested anymore… I feel like my time is up in your world. You still haven't been over here, and I don't want to continue wasting my time. I can have any man I want but I choose to want you, so I am being patient. I don't like where we are.

Text message received from Jayville:

Chill out. Relax. Aint nothing out here. It seems like you are chasing something

Text message sent to Jayville:

I am not chasing anything. It just seems like you're not into me anymore. I hardly see you now and talk to you.

Text message received from Jayville:

You just got out a whole divorce. Focus on the level up.

Text message sent to Jayville:

I am focused though

I sent him a voice note expressing how I felt and telling him that I am moving on. I am so tired of settling with him. He never responded to the voice note. So, that is that I am going to just continue to focus on Kai and myself. I am so happy I hired a Life Coach because he really is helping me with accountability. I am in full self-discovery and self-awareness mode. It is best I just let him go and end this toxic situationship.

***

"Hey Mom." I answered.

"What you and Kai up to?" She asked.

"Nothing, Kai taking a nap. What you up to?" I asked.

"About to cook soon. So, what's going on with Kai Daddy? You still haven't heard from him?" She asked.

"I am so glad you brought him up because that just reminded me. This Dude is behind on his car note and he still hasn't re-financed the car. Which means, my name is still on the car. He is affecting my credit. My credit score dropped over 70 points. I had no idea he was even behind." I told her.

"Are you serious?" She asked.

"YES! I am so serious, and I don't understand how he is even behind. He isn't helping me with Kai. He hasn't given me a dollar for him. I am paying this daycare by myself $520 a month. I am counting down for Kai to start kindergarten at this point. I just don't understand how he is sleeping at night knowing he is shitting on us. It just feels like I was never even married to him or with him all those years." I replied.

"I am in shock. I can't believe Bama either. But, do you plan on giving him your number and talking to him?" She asked.

"He doesn't need my number. We can continue to communicate through email." I told her.

"Okay, now that isn't being mature. You have a child with him, and you still must co-parent with him. The man is just hurt, and this is how he is dealing with it. I pray you both get it together for Kai's sake." She said.

"I just don't know Mom. It really hurt me the way he is dealing with his son and there is no excuse for that. On top of that to see how he is ruining my credit by being behind on the car note. He isn't even following the court order from the divorce. He was supposed to have that car out of my name thirty days after the divorce. We are going on six months. I have been so nice to him. I could have towed that car away or had them pick it up by now." I explained.

"Yes, well you know he is doing that out of spite to hurt you. Maybe he really doesn't have it. Do you think he can afford the car?" she asked.

"Mom, he is a man. I refuse to make anymore excuses for him. I am sorry I just can't." I answered.

"What's going on with Jayville?" She asked.

"Ugh!! Were not talking right now." I replied.

"Whhhaaatttt? Really? What happened?" she inquired.

"I just felt like he is seeing someone else and wasn't into me anymore. It just wasn't fun anymore. Then he keeps telling me to focus on healing, blah, blah, blah... He keeps saying the same shit to me when I bring up my feelings or the reality of our situation. I am just tired of it." I responded.

"He full of excuses huh? I tell you this. If a man really wants you, no excuse in the world would stop that man. Continue to work on yourself and it will come in time." She advised.

"Yes, that what I have been doing. I am just focusing on myself. I mean its hard to shake Jayville because I think about him every day. I still feel like he is my soul mate because of how we aligned together. But I know he isn't reciprocating the energy I am giving him. He just looks at me as an emotional, whiny, cry baby." I suggested.

"Baby, you can't force a man to want you or into anything. If he isn't ready, he just isn't ready. You must let him be. He knows that you are a good woman, but he isn't ready. You should respect him for not telling you sweet lies like the rest of these jokers be out here doing." She said.

"Yes, you are right. That is true too." I agreed.

Damn, now my Mom got me in my feelings thinking about Jayville again. She is right he is telling me and being honest with me. I guess I feel like he should've said all that from the beginning. If the expectation was set from the beginning then I wouldn't have given him my body, mind, and soul. Now I am trying to gain all that back. I hate love at this point because its so hard to control what the heart desires.

***

After the conversation I had with my Mom, I decided to reach out to Kai's Father and give him my number. I mean we need to co-exist either way. We do have a child together and we were married at one point. I advised him to give me a call so we can talk. I do need to speak with him about the car situation anyway.

"Hey" I answered.

"What's up?" Bama asked.

"I just think we need to stop with the games and be able to talk like adults." I suggested.

"You were the one on the games. Why you couldn't give me your number?" He asked.

"I mean you have my number now, so let's move on." I suggested.

"How is Kai doing?" He asked.

"Kai is doing good. He is getting so big and talking better." I replied.

"I do want to see him Friday." He suggested.

"What is going on with the car? I notice its still in my name and you are behind on the car note." I asked.

"U left me fucked up. I been fucked up out here. I got to get my credit together before I can re-finance." He answered.

"What do you mean, I left you fucked up?" I asked.

"When you moved out and left, I was stranded. You knew I couldn't afford that house by myself. You left me in a jam. Believe me I want your name off the car just as bad as you do." He answered.

"So, you are blaming me? You moved out the house two weeks after I left." I replied.

"Yes, because I couldn't afford it." He stated.

"Before I left, I helped you catch up your car note because you were falling behind. I didn't leave you fucked up. You aren't giving me any money for Kai or his daycare. I am doing this by myself. I have not put you on child support. You out here living freely and there should be no excuse. If you need to work two or three jobs than, that's what you should be doing." I told him.

"Here we go again. Okay, I am not about to go through this with you. I provide for my son." He said.

"Are you serious right now?" I asked.

"Look just make sure I see Kai on Friday." He demanded before hanging up the phone.

***

"Hi Mike!" I answered.

"How are you? How was your week?" Life coach Mike asked.

"It has been okay. I talked to Kai's Father." I replied.

"Are you still communicating with him through email only?" He asked.

"No, I gave him my number and we talked." I told him.

"That is major progress. I am happy you made that step. How do you feel about it?" He asked.

"Initially, I felt great about it. I felt mature and like I was ready to turn over a new leaf with co-parenting. But then…." I paused.

"Then what?" Life Coach asked.

"Once I heard his voice and felt his energy… I realized that I am not ready to deal with him. like I need more time.

I asked him about the car status, and he started pointing the finger blaming me. He was saying that I left him fucked up. Its like he still isn't being accountable for anything. He is still pointing the finger and blaming me. He still hasn't had a reality check and I can no longer tolerate his victim behavior. I dealt with that behavior for too many years. It just gave me a mental flashback on the reasons why I left. I can't find no excuse for him. He is aware of what he is doing, and he doesn't care because he blames me for leaving him. Like hello, I am raising a child here by myself. What about me?! No one cares about me!" I responded with tears crawling down my face.

"I understand." He responded before I cut him off from speaking.

"I am so tired of everyone always treating me like I am the problem. I dealt with that with my Father, ex-husband, and now Jayville. What am I doing wrong? I am so tired of this shit!" I yelled in the phone.

"Now, please relax. I understand the emotions that are coming over you, but I need you to relax. Your healing is not about them. It is not about how anyone sees you or value you. It is all about you. It is all about how you value yourself, what you will or will not tolerate. It starts within you. You must set these boundaries and expectations from the beginning when dealing with people. As you notice, you are the one that is being affected by it. They're still living their lives and living in their sin. You want to live with a clear conscious and heart. You are going to have to learn to forgive and how to protect your energy. That is the only way these people that hurt you can no longer continue to hurt you. Do you understand what I am suggesting to you?" he asked.

I nodded my head in the phone, wiped my tears and responded "Yes".

"Now, going forward we will work on your present. I have heard enough about your past. I want to move you forward with a new mindset." He told me.

"Okay, I agree. I am ready to let my past go. There is too much pain there and I am tired of reliving it." I told him.

***

Friday has finally arrived. At first, I wasn't going to allow Bama to see Kai but after speaking with my Life Coach I changed my mind. No matter how I feel about him, Kai loves his Dad. I know for a fact he missed his Dad. I will never want to be that kind of Mom to my child. I can't raise a boy into a man.

"Daddy!" Kai screamed out the window.

"Hey lil man!" Bama responded.

He opened the car door and took Kai out his car seat. He was holding him outside the car, admiring how big he got in such short time.

"Can he spend a night with me?" He asked me.

"I really want to see the inside of your place first." I suggested.

"So, what are you saying? My place aint in good enough condition for my son?" he asked.

All I can think in my head is, here we go again. This man is always trying to start an argument out of anything.

"No, that is not the case. I just want to see where he will be sleeping. If that is okay with you." I replied.

"No, its not okay with me. I don't want you seeing inside my place." He responded and then walked off towards his building with Kai in his hand.

All I can think in that moment is what Life Coach Mike

was saying to me. I was not going to allow him to take control over me. So, I just simply drove off. The old me would have gotten out the car and still followed him inside. The new me is focused on a peace of mind.

It does feel so weird not having Kai with me. I never imagined I would ever be dropping my son off or Bama being a weekend Dad to Kai. I am praying that he stays consistent and steps it up financially. My focus now is him not failing his son like he failed me as a Husband. I have faced and accepted what we have become. Our relationship is dead and will never rekindle. I just want to have a positive, healthy, co-parenting relationship. Kai is so smart, and he is paying attention. He is aware of what is going on without me saying. I am praying for Bama to renew is mind and way of thinking. I am praying the same for myself because that is the only way this co-parenting relationship will work.

***

For the first time I was able to face myself. I was able to understand where my underlying issues originated from. I never considered how my relationship with my Father played a major role with what I accept from a Man. I was able to finally forgive my Father. I was able to heal from my childhood pain. I was able to accept that my past doesn't define me.

CHAPTER 7

LOVING MYSELF

"Girlll!!! I can't wait to make a trip up there!" I told Punkin.
"Yes, best friend you need to make that trip back up here to the A." She agreed.
"It's nowhere like Atlanta in America. I promise you that." I told her.
"How long you been gone now?" She asked.
"I been gone for about three years, but you know I am planning to come back up there in two weeks." I answered.
"YESS!! We are going to have so much fun! You still haven't celebrated your divorce. You know we must turn up for that." She suggested.
"Damn, you are so right! I haven't properly celebrated! I love your family so much!" I said.
"Yes, we love you too. You know we are family" She assured me.
"Aww, I love you guys too. I love how close you guys are. I never had that for real growing up. That's what I admire about you guys so much. The unity and support you all have for each other no matter what. I Love your Mom so much!" I told her.
"Aww you know my Mama love you too" She said.
"Friend, I feel like I been so selfish lately. I am always talking about my problems, complaining, and shit. How have you been doing? What's been going on with you? I been so lost in my own world" I explained.
"You are always here for me, I am happy that I was able to be here for you." She replied.
"Oh my gosh Sis, you are going to make me cry. I feel like you the only one that really understands me. Thanks, so much Sis." I said.
"And that on Periona! ha-ha" She laughed and we both laughed together.

"On the real I had to surrender it all back to God. I have been neglecting him and he got my full attention now. I don't want to ever loose sight on him again." I told her.

"Amen, that's the only way!" She responded.

"Yes Ma'am" I said.

"So, you still haven't heard from Jayville?" She asked.

"Nope!" I answered.

"Wow, I'm shocked. I just don't see him walking away from a Badd bitch! I mean a Bad Bitch on her shit. He will dumb as hell too. Most boss niggaz want a boss bitch, unless he one of those with low self esteem that feeds off weak bitches!" She concluded.

"EXACTLY SIS! But, hey I have accepted what it is." I told her.

"You'll be alright, you do need time to continue to heal and enjoy yourself. I am so proud of you Sis." She said.

"Thanks Hun! I appreciate you so much!" I told her.

We talked for about an hour more about life and how far we have come. Punkin has been my ride or die friend through it all. God don't bless you with too many friends like this.

***

Date day for me and Kai. Today, we are going out for breakfast, to the children museum, and to Chuck e cheeses. I am probably more excited than he is. I love to eat and have fun. One way to my heart is through food. Hopefully, my next Husband will know how to cook.

Since I divorced his Dad, I want to make sure we grow a strong tight mother and son bond. So, it is so important that I spend valuable time with my son. In these specials moments we are creating memories together. This will be instilled in him, and he will never suffer from having

"Mommy issues." Each day I realize how important it is for the next person I am with to love my son like their own.

***

Wow, I cannot believe I am going into my last life coaching session. The eight weeks went by fast. I am not interested in renewing the services. Mike was a blessing for me, and I am grateful for his services. We did seven sessions over the phone, so our last session will be done in person. I am excited to finally meet the man behind the voice.

I just arrived at his business location and it is in a nice upscale corporate building. I wonder how much money he makes as a Life Coach. I am considering possibly adding coaching to my marketing business. His sessions are pricey and that why I can't afford to renew. It was an invest for real to hire him, but it was worth it. I feel so much calmer and in control. Here he comes to the door. Wow, he looks a lot shorter than he does on his website and fatter. I can only assume that life is good.

"I am so happy to finally meet you Navia! How are you? Was the drive okay to get here?" He asked.

"I am happy to finally match your voice with your face, I am doing well. The drive wasn't that bad, thanks for asking." I answered.

"Here have a seat here and make yourself comfortable. Make sure your phone is on silent. I really can't stand when a session is interrupted due to a notification, which can lead to throwing off the session." He said.

"Yes Sir, I understand completely. This is a nice office and building. Is it really expensive to lease an office here?' I asked. The nosiness in me just had to ask.

"Thanks, yes it isn't cheap. There are lawyers, plastic surgeons, marketing firms and other therapist located in this building as well." He answered.

That wasn't the answer I was hoping for, but I guess it will do.

"Oh okay, that is nice." I said.

"So, talk to me. How has it been going? How was your week?" he asked.

"It has been going great! I had a day date with my son two days, and we had a blast. I am in a great space." I answered.

"To see the confidence in you when you answered that question was impactful. Some people can say they are doing great and you are able to see the misery in their eyes. I believe you and can feel your positive energy. I feel so proud hearing you say that and how far you have come with self-discovery. I am looking at notes from our first session and you were indeed really broken, lost and confused." He admitted.

"Yes, I have came along way with your advice and guidance." I told him.

"Thanks, but you did all the work." He said.

"ha-ha, yes that's true! You have contributed to directing me back on track with my spirituality. I must give my Mother credit as well. You both pointed out that most important area in my life where I lost track of. I turned away from God and felt resentment towards him. I stopped praying, meditating, reading my bible. I just gave up on feeding my spirit. I am so thankful for God's grace. It's amazing how God will use people over your life. I am happy that my relationship with God is strengthening everyday and getting back on track. I can admit when God is missing in your life its hard to feel that peace. You will always feel miserable and like something is missing. You will never feel complete." I said.

"Okay, Navia you are preaching. You are taking me to church. Your growth within two months is amazing." He said.

"Aww, thanks" I responded.

"So, whatever was the outcome with Jayville? I noticed you haven't mentioned him in the last two sessions." He asked.

"Yes, I haven't. I have finally decided to let Jayville go. It was a hard decision for me. I was caught between knowing when to be patient and knowing when to let go. I decided to let go and accept that no matter how I feel. We will never be together. I still don't know if that is the right answer because he is my soul mate in my heart, and we could've been a power couple. I know for right now this is what is best." I explained.

"It seems like you are really done with him. How does it make you feel, letting him go?" He asked.

"Geesh, that was the worst pain to ever endure or accept. I know that it is the best for me to move on. It has been over one month now since we have talked. He only made one attempt to contact me since, the day after I sent him a message telling him I'm moving on. He sent me a YouTube video link of this classic love song. It was referring to holding on, but that was it. He hasn't tried to reach back out to me, and it hurts that he hasn't. I never thought it would have been so easy for him to walk away. I guess I believed my own fairytale. I am still healing from him and this heartbreak every day. I take full accountability and I am in a way better space now." I answered.

"That is really mature of you and shows that you are indeed intune within yourself to be able to accept the reality of the situation. Good for you to know your worth. What you deserve and what you don't deserve. That is the hardest thing for most women to accept. Give me an update on Bama. How is the co-parenting going now?" He asked.

"The co-parenting is going. We have come along way within the last couple of months. He has really been consistent with getting him now. I am no longer arguing with him or trying to be difficult. I just want what is best for my son Kai. We still are at odds over the car though. I am still trying to figure that situation out. Every time I ask him about it, he just tells me he is working on it. It has a big impact on my credit score. That is pretty much it outside of that." I answered.

"I am glad to hear that you guys are on a common ground with the co-parenting. That is good you are no longer arguing with him or trying to be difficult. The car situation will work itself out. Continue to pray on it and God will give you clarity on your next move." He suggested.

"Amen Sir! I agree and that is all I can do at this point is leave it in God's hand. I am in such a beautiful space now. I am finally loving myself. I just want to spread that energy to everyone. I wish happiness on everyone. Happiness is the biggest high!" I said.

"ha-ha, I am loving it and I feel that energy from you. You are right! Happiness is the greatest high to experience. I feel comfortable releasing you Navia. You have been my favorite client thus far. It is really rare to come across clients who are willing to accept accountability and successfully work towards change." He said.

"Thank you! That really meant a lot!" I replied.

The last session with my life coach was the most important one for me. I was able to identify how broken I was just two months ago. Evaluating how weak I was during that short time ago, it reminds me to never allow myself to enter back into that mental state. Mike sent me all our recorded calls, assignments, and he shared his folder with me. I was impressed that he had so much files on me. It just really shows how great he is, at what he does. I would've never imaged that he had such great detail notes on each session. He sent it to me to as a reflection tool to rate my growth. I am so grateful that I made that decision to invest in myself. This decision has impacted my life for a lifetime. I will take advantage of everything I have learned throughout the sessions to stay on track.

***

I am so happy to be back in Atlanta. Atl is truly the Black Hollywood. There are so many black successful entrepreneurs here. I have done a lot of traveling around America and there is no where else like Atlanta for Blacks. You really have a higher chance of living a better life in Atlanta. If you really want it too though, because there are still some people that are struggling here too. There is no excuse if you put your mind to it.

Every time I come in town, I stay with my Bestie if she is single. When she is in a relationship, I book a hotel. I am very big on respect and I would never feel comfortable staying with her and her man. Even if it is just for two or three days. And she is Single! Yay!! We are about to have so much fun, officially celebrating my divorce!

"Open the door Bitch!" I yelled outside the door while banging on it.

"Is that my Bestie!" She yelled, before she opened the door.

We embraced each other with the tightest hug. I had to catch myself from crying. Only because I am so emotional at times and I haven't seen her since my divorce.

"I got your drink waiting on you right here!" She yelled, as she passed me the drink.

"You weren't playing when you said you were going to have me wasted, ha-ha-ha" I said.

"Damn, sure wasn't!" she answered.

"So, where are we going tonight? I haven't been to a club in so long. It has been maybe two years." I told her.

"Okay, we do a lounge. I be forgetting your bougie, hood classy ass!" She laughed.

"ha-ha, you right about that" I laughed.

"Okay, let's relax and unwind. I know I been killing your ears with my problems. What has been going on with you?" I asked.

We talked and caught up with everything. I was finally able to catch up with her life. She has been sparring me her problems to listen to mine. I was so happy to be able to finally be her ear. It is a good thing to here other people situations too. We drank the entire night. I was so drunk by the time we started getting ready to hit this lounge I didn't even know if I still was even interested in going. This is how you know when your age is catching up with you.
***

Party time! Me and Bestie was dressed from head to toe. Were botch petite and chocolate, so you know we were giving these Niggaz toothaches looking at us. I seen so many old faces and a lot of new faces. My vision wasn't all the way clear because I was already wasted before I even got to the lounge. We had so much fun, it didn't feel legal. I haven't had that much fun in years. I notice this guy from across the lounge by the bar watching me. I mean he was watching me the entire night. It got to a point that I was immune   to   him   watching   me.

145

"Bestie, that nigga got his eye on you!" Punkin said.

"Yes, its hard to not notice. His scary ass aint buy me a drink or nothing. Hahaha" I laughed.

"Oh okay, I forgot yo ass been out the city for a while. That's Pablo. He from Macon, but I heard the nigga is paid. He a boss type Nigga. You know the kind you like. Bitches be so thirsty over him. I am surprised aint no bitch in his face now." She said.

"Well, that explains why he is just staring. Welp, I am not about to be thirsty over him. So, he can just keep staring. Them chasing days are over for me. Jayville took all that shit from me" I said.

"Bahahaha Bitch you crazy" She laughed.

"I am so serious. I can never look at these Niggaz the same after him. Shit between him and Bama. Them fuckers ruined my heart." I said.

"Fuck them! Let's get back out on the dance floor!" She said.

Punkin grabbed my hand and walked me back to the dance floor. It was perfect timing because they were playing one of my favorite artist Jhene Aiko, bullshit! I sang the life out that song! This night was so epic. It was such a great way to start off my first night back in Atlanta. As we were walking out the club, the Pablo dude appeared out of nowhere.

"Good night Miss Lady" He said.

"Hi" I responded.

"Are you from here?" He asked.

"Are you going to go straight into the twenty-one questions without asking me my name?" I asked him

"Excuse me, You a feisty one. What's your name sweetheart?" he asked.

"Nay. What's yours?" I asked him.

"Sean but I go by Pablo." He answered.

"Nice to meet you Sean." I replied.

"Nice to meet you Nay!" He said.

"Where are you from? You don't seem like an Atlanta chick." He said.

"Oh really!" I answered.

"Yes, I would be shocked if you were, your swag is different." He said.

"Okay, well I guess that is a compliment. I am from Florida, but I did grow up in Atlanta. I no longer live here though." I told him.

"Wow, I knew you weren't from here. How long are you in town?" he asked.

I'll be here until Monday" I answered.

"Damn, you just did a drive by." He said

"ha-ha, I guess so!" I laughed.

"Can you bless me with your number?" he asked.

I am still really intoxicated trying to have a sober conversation which is beyond hard for me right now. But, did he just say "bless me" with your number. I never heard that one before.

"Just give me yours." I asked.

He gave me his number and asked if he can see me before I leave. I am thinking, I need to call you first. I was so relieved that he was out of my face. That conversation was the hardest to have.

"Do you think he knew hoe fucked up I was?" I asked Punkin.

"Girl, I forgot you were drunk. You held your composure great." She said.

"Really?" I asked for clarity.

"Yes, and he likes you. I seen how his eyes was connecting with your eyes. That nigga is paid Sis! Are you going to call him?" She asked.

"Shitt…I hope I even remember him in the morning." We both laughed.

"I know that's right! I felt like I was celebrating my divorce too. I had so much fun. It felt like old times foreal." She said.

"Best fucking night ever. I must repent in the morning. Oh God I am so sorry for getting so drunk Lord, please forgive me." I started praying to God.

"Girl, you better stop that shit! God aint listening to your drunk ass right now! Bahahaha" she laughed.

"Stop it Punkin" I yelled.

"Yep, time to go home. Before your ass start crying in shit. We can't even go to an after party. We are going straight home!" She said.

***

"My fucking head hurt so bad right now" I told Punkin as I sat down on the couch.

"Girl, mine too. Damn, we should've went to Waffle house after. That would've helped. We didn't eat enough. I think I got some Gatorade or Pedialyte in my pantry." She suggested.

"I hope you do because this shit got me feeling like I am about to die from a brain explosion!" I said.

"Why are you so damn dramatic? Hahaha… I can't with you Nay! I promise!" She said.

"What, I am being so serious right now. I know I said I wanted to get lit but damn! I still have a son to live for!" I said.

"Bitch, get out now!" She said jokingly.

"ha-ha, what!" I laughed.

"We both have kids to live for! Anyways you going to hit Pablo up?" she asked.

"Am I going to hit who up?" I asked.

"Bitch don't play dumb. Fine ass, paid ass Pablo?" She asked again.

"Girl, you know I totally forgot about him. My head hurt so damn bad. Was he fine for real because I remember that name but I don't remember how he looks." I asked her.

"Yes, he fine as shit!" She answered.

"Describe him to me again. I really don't remember. Was he tall? You already know I don't like no Man under 6ft. I don't care how much money they have." I told her.

"He is tall, brown, and fine! Call his ass to see for yourself. That nigga was gazing in your eyes and shit. You need to at least have a friend talk to. Its not like he lives in Florida anyway. He can be your long-distance boo." She said.

"Well, thanks for the recommendation, ha-ha" I laughed.

"And you can get some money, gifts, trips out of him too." She suggested.

"Punkin! Yo ass! I just don't know if I am ready to have a male friend right now. I am so focused on me and I still haven't gotten over Jayville." I said.

"Here we go again. Bitch you aint gone never get over that nigga if you don't start exploring your options. Jayville living his best life. That nigga probably laid up with a Bitch now and that what you need to be thinking every time you think about him!" she said.

"Damn, you right! Geesh that was thug love right there!" I laughed.

"Now text Pablo." She insisted.

"Okay, Mama! Damn!" I replied

Text message sent to Pablo:
Hi
Text message received from Pablo:
I was wondering if you were going to hit me.
Text message sent to Pablo:
Do you know who this is?
Text message received from Pablo:
Of course, Nay 1 been waiting on you all day.
Text message sent to Pablo:
Lol
Text message received from Pablo:
I want to learn more about you. I would love to take you to lunch.
Text message sent to Pablo:
Idk
Text message received from Pablo:
Just let me know. I would love to see you again.
"Girl, he saying he want to take me to lunch. He is really going hard." I told Punkin.
"That's what up. What did you say? Are you going to go?" She asked.
"I told him I don't know. Because I really don't. I came here to spend time with you and celebrate my divorce not find love." I told her.
"That is a good point" She agreed.
"I'll see him before I leave. Just not today." I said.
"I found Pedialyte. That shit is so nasty, but it helps with hangovers. You still want some?" Punkin asked.
"Yes, Ma'am my head is still on fire, trust me. I will drink it." I responded.
We just relaxed the rest of the day, with no energy to leave the house. We brought my first night in a bang and were to old to repeat that night back to back.

Text message received from Pablo:
How are you doing?
Text message sent to Pablo:
Ok and you?
Text message received from Pablo:
I was looking forward to taking you out today
Text message sent to Pablo:
I'm tired
Text message received from Pablo:
I understand. Maybe tomorrow.
Text message sent to Pablo:
Well see
***

Day three in Atlanta, and I am not looking forward to going back home. I do miss Kai like crazy, but he is in great hands with my Mom. I am so blessed to have her support with him. I have no idea what I would do without it. Especially as a single mother, we need a break from time to time. Boys are so much work and they are so busy body. I know it is only going to get more challenging with time.
"Hey Mom" I answered the phone.
"How is it in Atlanta? You having fun?" She asked.
"I am having a blast. How is Kai?" I asked.
"He is good. Here he goes" She said and then handed him the phone.
"Hi Mommy!" Kai yelled into the phone.
"Hey Baby! What are you doing?" I asked him.
"Watching tv." He answered.
"What are you watching?" I asked him
"Paw patrol Mommy" He said.
"I should've known. I miss you! Do you miss Mommy?" I asked.

"Yes, I miss you and love you Mommy." He answered.

"Aww I love you too Baby" I told him before he gave the phone back to my Mom.

"Enjoy your time!" My Mom said.

"No doubt. See you guys soon! Love you!" I told her.

"Love you too." She responded.

Mommy guilt is so real. Now I just want to rush back home to be with Kai. I miss my baby so much now. I couldn't imagine my life without him. I'll be forever thankful to the Most High for allowing me and Bama to create that beautiful blessing.

***

"Let's hit the Ocean bar today" Punkin came into the living room saying.

"Sure, that sounds good. Aw shit look who just hit me?" I told her.

Text message received from Pablo:

How are you?

Text message sent to Pablo:

Hi, I'm doing good. U?

Text message received from Pablo:

Blessed

"Pablo! You should invite him to the bar." Punkin suggested.

"Now that is a good idea. He can buy or drinks, Bahahaha" I told her.

"Exactly!" She agreed.

Text message received from Pablo:

What the rest of your day looking like?

Text message sent to Pablo:

Me and my Bestie hitting the Ocean bar. Your welcome to see me there.

Text message received from Pablo:

Aight, around when?

"Punkin, when we going up there?" I asked.

"We bout to leave soon. Tell him an hour" She answered.

"Okay!" I said.

Text message sent to Pablo:

In the next 2hrs

Text message received from Pablo:

Aight

I know Punkin said one hour, but that didn't sound right. Especially since she wasn't even dressed yet. I am a little nervous about seeing this guy again. I am not ready to even have a friend, but I guess it won't hurt.

***

We arrived at Ocean bar just at two hours. My timing couldn't have been more perfect. We pulled up the same time Pablo pulled up. Pablo pulled up in a nice new black on black G-wagon. Punkin was right, he was fine as hell. Oh my gosh! How did I not remember that damn face? I was really drunk because he is the opposite of the description that I had in my head. He was tall, dark brown, Chinese small eyes, nice athletic built, and he was tatted up. I love tattoos and small eyes, especially being that I have big eyes. He looked like a professional ball player. Maybe he is an ex player. Now, I am just curious and feeling like Inspector Gadget.

"Hey Beautiful! Your even better looking in the daytime." He suggested.

"Thanks!" I blushed.

"Where do you all want to sit?" Punkin asked.

"It doesn't matter to me" Pablo responded.

"Okay, I'll let you two decide. My friend just pulled up. I

am going to go meet him outside. Well be back in soon."
Punkin said.

"Okay, cool" I told her.

Me and Pablo walked to a table in the back of the bar, kind of ducked off. I do remember Punkin saying he had a lot of groupies and he was well known. I didn't want to be on front street with him. At this point I know nothing about him. He can be a damn Drug Lord for all I know. The first few minutes after we sat down felt so weird. He kept staring at me without saying anything. This gave me a flashback of the club. I feel like my memory was coming back to me.

"Are you going to sit here and not say anything?" I asked.

"I am so amazed at your beauty. You are so naturally pretty. Look at you... You are rocking your real hair, no make-up, no big ass eyelashes." He said.

"Thanks, that's great observation" I said.

Oh my gosh he is making me extremely shy right now. I hope Punkin hurries back. I hope she didn't do this shit on purpose. Let me text her ass.

Text message sent to Bestie Punkin:

Wya?

Text message received from Bestie Punkin:

Brb

What the fuck. Her ass left. Ima kill her. She set my ass up! Dammit.

"U okay?" Pablo asked.

"Yes." I responded.

I felt like I was about to have an anxiety attack and I didn't even know I had anxiety. I was not ready for a date quite yet. Now, I am placed on the spot.

"What do you want to drink?" he asked

"I'll take a lemon drop Martini" I told him.

"Nice, are you hungry?" he asked.

"No, thanks!" I answered.

"Okay" he said.

He signaled the waitress and placed our drink order. I noticed he has two phones. It made me think of Jayville and I don't even know why I am still thinking about him. Lord clear my thoughts.

"Tell me a little about yourself. Do you have any kids?" he asked.

"Yes, I have a little boy. Do you have any" I asked.

"Yes, I have a son as well. How old are you? If you don't mind me asking." He asked.

"No, I don't mind, I am thirty-one. You?" I asked.

"Wow, you look damn good. I thought you were still in your twenties. I just couldn't guess if it was the mid-twenties or not. I am thirty-five." He answered.

"Okay, that not bad. You are only four years older than me." I replied.

"That's perfect in my book. I can't get passed your beauty. What's your ethnicity?" He asked.

"Caribbean, Jamaican, Indian, Bahamian" I answered.

"Makes sense." He said.

"Thanks, so are you married, divorced, in a relationship?" I asked.

"I am single, but I do date from time to time. I never been married." He answered.

"Thanks for being honest. I hate when men can't admit that they are dating." I told him.

"I believe in giving people a chance to make the best decision for themselves. If you cannot date me because I am dating someone else, then I allowed you that choice."

He said.

"I have to agree with you. That is so real" I said.

"I see no ring on your finger. Are you seeing anyone?" He asked.

"Nope, I am single." I told him.

"Damn, I met you at the right time." he said.

The fact that he said that to me with a straight face, it scared me and turned me on at the same time.

"Yes, I guess you did. Only time will tell." I said.

"What do you do for a living?" he asked.

"I am a dancer." I said.

"Oh okay, so you dance in Florida?" He asked.

"I am so playing with you. I have my own marketing consultant business and I work in the fintech industry." I replied.

"Damn, you beautiful and you smart. You seem like a great catch. I am surprised you're not married with three kids." He jokingly said.

"Well, I was waiting for you to ask me if I was ever married but you assumed, I wasn't. I am divorced." I told him.

"I am sorry to hear that. How long were you together?" he asked.

"We were together almost nine years and married for five years." I answered.

"Damn, that was for some time." He said.

"Yep, so what do you enjoy doing for fun?" I asked him.

I didn't want to spend the next hour talking about my failed marriage. I am so tired of talking about it and thinking about it.

"I love to travel, read, learn new things, make money, you know all that good shit." He answered.

"What about you?" He asked

"The exact same thing. The only thing I would add is spending time with my son and write." I told him.

"Damn, I forgot to add that too. I enjoy my Jr as well." He said.

"How old is your son?" I asked

"He is ten years old, he lives in Macon, Georgia with his Mom. That is where I am from. I try to see him and spend time with him at least once a month. We talk everyday and our bond is indescribable." He explained.

"That's so dope, I love hearing that!" I told him.

"How old is your blessing?" He asked.

"Kai will be turning four soon." I replied.

"Oh, okay you have a terrible toddler, ha-ha" he laughed.

"Yes, that is exactly right. Do you want anymore kids?" I asked.

"Depends, with the right woman. Matter of fact with my future wife. I never wanted to be the guy with baby mamas all over the place." He admitted.

"Amen to that. I waited for marriage to have my son and it still didn't work. So, I understand." I told him.

"Would you be open to re-marrying and having more kids?" He asked me.

"Of course, I haven't given up on love. I am just a lot wiser with my heart. I want a little girl so bad." I replied.

"I want a little girl too." He agreed.

"Aww, I can tell she would be spoiled." I said.

"That's fasho. Do you want another drink?" he asked.

"Sure!" I told him.

Now I am looking at my phone like, where is Punkin it's an hour later.

Text message sent to Bestie Punkin:

Girl, you okay?

Text message received from Bestie Punkin:
We outside.
Text message sent to Bestie Punkin:
K
I felt relieved knowing that she is okay and outside.
"You are very intellectual. These broads out here nowadays can't hold a conversation for shit." He laughed.
"Hahaha, thanks!" I said.
Pablo surprised me. I thought he was going to be a hood, worldly minded type of guy. Most men these days are focused on materialistic things, artificial looking women, and keeping up the stereotype of whatever is in style. He was pretty dope. We talked for about another hour before Punkin and her friend guy came to the table. At that point we both were ready to go. Since, Punkin daughters were with their Dad. We decided to take it back to her place and chill. We enjoyed more drinks and had a great time. We played spades, and just sat around talking about conspiracies. It was so much fun. Especially since it was my last night in Atlanta. This trip was so refreshing and needed. This trip showed me that there is still hope for me in the love department and how important it is to seize every moment.
"Well, I am about to head out, thanks for inviting me over." Pablo stood up and said.
"I'll walk with you outside." I told him.
I walked with him and we stood outside his car for another hour talking. I can tell he really was feeling me and wanted to invite me over to his crib. I would have told him no! I just realized I still haven't asked him what he does for a living. It is like every time I am about to ask him the conversation shift gears. We gave each other a hug before

he departed. He smelled so good. Whatever cologne he had on was the truth because it still smelled amazing hours later.

***

"Bestie, don't go!" Punkin came in the room yelling.

"I know it, I had so much fun. This is so hard for me to leave. If I didn't have Kai, I wouldn't go back." I assured her.

"Well the turn up was real! I wish you could've got some dick though. That would help you snap out of that Jayville spell your under." She said.

"ah-ha, what!!" I couldn't hold back my laughter.

"That's right, you heard me!" She jokingly said.

"I promise I love you!" I told her.

"Are you going to continue to talk to Pablo?" she asked.

"I don't know. We'll see." I told her.

"You are so weird." She suggested.

"Look, I am not getting my hopes up anymore. Actions with time will proof it all!" I told her.

"True!" She agreed.

Text message received from Pablo:

Good morning Beautiful

Text message sent to Pablo:

Good morning

Text message received from Pablo:

I'm outside!

Text message sent to Pablo:

Outside where?

Text message received from Pablo:

Punkin building. Come outside.

"Punkin! Punkin!" I yelled.

"Why are you yelling my name. Sounding like one of damn

kids." She asked.

"Tell me why this nigga outside!" I yelled.

"What Nigga? Pablo?" She asked.

"Yes! Bitch!" I told her.

"So, go outside!" She suggested.

"Who does that though?" I asked.

"Didn't you just say some shit about a Nigga got to show you in actions if its real. Hahaha!" She laughed.

"That's not funny. And seems kind of crazy to me. He is lucky, I already have clothes on." I told her.

"He probably just trying to see you before you hit the road. I doubt he meant anything by it. Loosen up some!" She said.

I made his ass wait about twenty minutes before I walked outside. I mean that is still not sitting right with me. Hold up! I think he left. Wait, is this him in this silver Bentley. Damn, this Nigga really paid. I walked over towards the car and opened the passenger door.

"Damn, you took long enough. You just woke up?" He asked.

I sat down, amazed at how nice his interior was.

"No, I was up packing. Why did you just pop up like that?" I asked.

"I wanted to see you and I knew you were leaving today. I just wanted to catch you before you left. You been on my mind all night." He said.

"That is nice and all but please don't ever do that again." I told him.

"Excuse me!" he said jokingly.

"Your excused." I said.

"I know you felt that connection, you can't tell me it was just me?" he asked.

160

I paused. I am no longer good with telling the difference of a Man telling me what I want to hear versus being real with what he is saying. Jayville messed me all up. I believed every word that nigga said. What if this nigga really means what he is saying? I just can't risk my heart anymore.

"I really don't know. It takes time to get to know people." I answered.

Yes, that is true, but I really like what I see and what I know so far." He said.

"Okay." I responded.

"Can we still talk and keep in touch?" He asked.

"Sure!" I responded.

We talked in his car for about thirty minutes. I can tell he didn't want me to leave. I just felt like he was ready to risk it all for me to stay. I am a Mother and I have my own life to attend back too. I just can't set myself up to be vulnerable again. Not right now at least, this is too early in the game. We hugged and he walked me back to the door and hugged me again.

"Please call me once you get on the road." He told me as he walked away.

"Girl! Seems like he is attached already, and he didn't even get any kitty kat yet." I told Punkin.

Punkin busted out laughing. "ha-ha-ha"

"Hush, I am foreal!" I said with a straight face.

"Well he is a good catch and you are a good catch too. I feel like it would be a perfect duo!" She suggested.

"I have to hit this road, let me get my stuff." I told her.

I finished packing my stuff up, before heading out. It is always hard leaving Punkin. We always have a ball together.
***

"Lord knows I have drunk my ass off and overdose on the

liquor. God please forgive your daughter. I will not drink to get drunk next time." I said aloud in the car headed back home. Debating if I should call Pablo. Id rather just text him.

Text message sent to Pablo:
Just wanted to let you know that I'm on the road back home
Text message received from Pablo:
Be safe on that road, hit me when you get home
Text message sent to Pablo:
Okay

I wonder how long he will keep up with communicating with me. I am quite sure he will forget about me by next weekend. He is too fine to still be worried about someone he just met that is out of state.

***

Two weeks later, surprisingly Pablo is still hanging around. He wants to get away from Atlanta and come visit me. I just don't know how I feel about that. I think he is dope but I am still not ready.

"Hey Hun" I answered Punkin.

"What you got going on over there?" she asked.

"Just chatting with Pablo. He wants to come up here to see me to get away. But I don't know." I told her.

"Here we go again. Just tell him to get a hotel and let him take you out. You don't have to sleep with him." She suggested.

"Well, I know that because I'm celibate. I just don't want to move fast, and he already showed me that he is Mr. Pop up on yo ass." I said jokingly.

"Well, you right about that one." She agreed.

"I just must pray about it and think about it some more. How are you and the girls?"

"We good. Just checking on you and Kai." She said.

"Okay, we love you!" I told her.

"We love you too!" she said before hanging up.

***

As, I lay here in my bed this morning and reflect. I am for the first happy with my life. I am so proud to be back intune within myself and my relationship with God. I am so intune that I will never allow myself to settle or lower my expectations. I must admit I was in a weak space, spiritually, emotionally, and mentally.

I turned from God and placed all my faith in Man. I learned that whenever you praise a man, more than God you will always loose. God will never leave you or forsaken you. It doesn't matter how many times you fall; God is always there to pick you right back up through repentance. I am so thankful for God's mercy and grace. I love God so much and I am so happy I surrendered and found my way back to him. God love is unconditional and everlasting. Therefore, I will always put my trust in God, and not Man. Thank you Lord for the lesson that turned into a blessing. I am Alive! I am finally at peace and in a happy space. For the first time since I can remember I am happy. It feels even more beautiful because, I am not happy over a man! In the past I always defined my happiness from a man. I may have finally met the one but only time will tell because I am leaning on God this time around for guidance through prayer.

(Knock knock…. Knock… knock knock at the door)

Its like seven in the morning. Who is that at my damn door? It couldn't be… Am I sleep walking or dreaming right now…Are my eyes playing tricks on me? I know damn well this is not JAYVILLE at my damn door.

Oh Wow, it is him and it looks like he has a gift in his hand for me. What in the fuckin World!

TO   BE   CONTINUED...

Here are more ways to Stay Connected:

If interested in talking with Dee please visit:
https://linktr.ee/authordevans

Please like me on Facebook:
@Authordeeevans
www.facebook.com/authordeeevans/

Follow me on Instagram:
@Authordevans

www.instagram.com/authordevans/

Subscribe to my YouTube channel:

www.youtube.com/c/LifeCoachDee7

Thanks for Reading and don't forget to Check out Part 2!

MORE BOOKS & JOURNALS FROM DEE

"Lies, Façade & Deceit: Life After a Toxic Marriage part 2"

"Rise up in Faith: Forgiveness & Repentance"

"Devotion, Inspiration & God's Word"

"God's Voice for Prayers: 45 Psalms & Prayers"

"30-Day Devotional & Inspiration for the Single Mom"

"Thoughts from a Black Woman"

"Lust, Pain & Love: A Poetry Collection"

"90-Day Gratitude Journal 4 Men"

"Her Price is far above Rubies: 90-day Self-Reflection Journal"

ABOUT THE AUTHOR

Dee Evans is a servant of the Most High, wife, and Mother. She is on a mission to write books to inspire, motivate, and uplift your spirit.
Dee is also a Book Publisher, Poet, 2xPodcaster, Life Coach, and Non-profit Consultant.

Check out Dee's Podcasts Streaming on Youtube & all major streaming sites:
"Dee Poetry & Inspiration Podcast" and "Black Girls in Faith Podcast"

If interested in sharing your story with the world through publishing please visit:
www.rise2write.com